KINDNESS
for
WEAKNESS

ALSO BY SHAWN GOODMAN

Something Like Hope

KINDNESS
for
WEAKNESS

• • •

SHAWN GOODMAN

DELACORTE PRESS

Text copyright © 2013 by Shawn Goodman
Jacket photograph copyright © 2013 by Alexander Shahmiri

All rights reserved. Published in the United States by Delacorte Press, an imprint of Random House Children's Books, a division of Random House, Inc., New York.

Delacorte Press is a registered trademark and the colophon is a trademark of Random House, Inc.

Visit us on the Web! randomhouse.com/teens
Educators and librarians, for a variety of teaching tools, visit us at RHTeachersLibrarians.com

Library of Congress Cataloging-in-Publication Data
Goodman, Shawn.
    Kindness for weakness / Shawn Goodman.—1st ed.
        p.   cm.
    Summary: A fifteen-year-old boy from an abusive home desperately seeking his older brother's love and approval starts pushing drugs for him and suffers the consequences.
    ISBN 978-0-385-74324-2 (hc : alk. paper)—ISBN 978-0-375-99102-8 (glb : alk. paper)—ISBN 978-0-307-98207-0 (ebook)—
ISBN 978-0-385-74325-9 (tr. pbk. : alk. paper)   [1. Brothers—Fiction. 2. Self-esteem—Fiction.   3. Drug dealers—Fiction.]   I. Title.
    PZ7.G61442Ki 2013   [Fic]—dc23   2012015772

The text of this book is set in 12-point Baskerville.
Book design by Vikki Sheatsley

Printed in the United States of America
10 9 8 7 6 5 4 3 2 1
First Edition

For Jenna

1

White-clad paramedics run alongside the gurney, guiding me through the electric gates of the facility and across the parking lot, where a helicopter waits. They are careful even though they're in a hurry, and I want to thank them, maybe tell them not to go to so much trouble for me, because I feel fine despite what has just happened. Also, it's been a long time since anyone has worried about me, and truth be told, it's a little embarrassing. One of the men puts his hand on mine and says, "Hang in there, buddy. You're going to make it. I swear you're going to be okay."

I want to say something to reassure him, but I can't talk. My breathing is thin and shallow, and it's all I can do to keep my eyes open and look at the helicopter blades hanging down at their tips, all wobbly and half-assed. I wonder how something so fragile-looking can fly, but then the rotor powers up and the blades become a cyclone beating down the air and flattening me to the gurney. The paramedics fold up the legs of the gurney and slide me into the helicopter.

"Just hold on, buddy," the guy says again. I try to smile to let him know I'm okay, but my face muscles don't work. I can move my eyes, though, and I look out the windows, which are all around. A tornado of dirt and leaves swirls outside, twigs and bugs and other dried-up things riding the currents of air.

And I'm excited, because for the first time I am flying.

2

In the beginning there is so much walking that I have holes in my shoes. Half the time I don't even know where I'm going or why. One more block, my body says, and the legs just carry out their orders, striding over cracked sidewalks, patches of trampled spring grass, and the occasional globe of dandelion fluff. These I kick sharply, trying to send each seed on its way so that it might float and drift and, eventually, find a nice place to live. It doesn't seem like such a stupid idea, until I see all the perfect lawns and realize I'm making a mess, adding ten or twenty more yellow flowers to be dug up and thrown away. So I quicken my pace and stop looking down.

Instead I watch the little kids playing outside the shingled two-story houses: boys and girls riding scooters and Big Wheels in the driveways, running around with dogs in fenced backyards. The kids shriek and laugh and chase each other with sticks. What would it be like to live that way, with a watchful German shepherd, a bicycle, and friends? To sprawl on an L-shaped couch in front of the bluish glow of a big-screen TV, a mother saying, "I'm going to the kitchen. How about some soda and a big bowl of popcorn?" Or maybe she would just touch the top of my head as a kind of gesture, a silent everyday way of saying, "Hey, kid, I love you."

Of course, all this thinking is crazy, because I don't live in one of those houses and never will. Even the little kids seem to understand this, because they stop playing and stand shoulder to shoulder, staring at me with serious little-kid faces, the kinds that show they recognize that something around them is wrong. Not dangerous, but different. Out of place. A friendless fifteen-year-old kid with nowhere to go. But as soon as I pass, they return to their games, shrieking and laughing and chasing each other around. They roll madly up and down the driveway on their Big Wheels, pebbles rattling inside cracked plastic mags, the unmistakable sound of things that are right and good. The sound of things that belong. I walk even faster and get the hell out of there.

3

It's two o'clock on a Sunday, and I head over to Dirk's Gym to see my big brother, Louis, who is nineteen and has his own apartment. Louis is only four years older than me, but he's pretty much an adult. He left home over a year ago, when Ron, my mom's boyfriend, moved in with us. "It's him or me," Louis said. My mother paced the edge of the living room, chewing her nails, smoking an unfiltered Camel; she did not say one word. That's when Louis packed his clothes in a couple of garbage bags. He gave me one of those quick thumping tough-guy hugs and pushed through the broken screen door. He never came back.

Dirk's is a really small place, but it's the only gym in Dunkirk, which itself is nowhere, a small town in western New York that's been quietly rusting on the shores of Lake Erie ever since the Allegheny-Ludlum and Roblin Steel plants closed. The front room of Dirk's is filled with trophies and posters of locals who have placed in bodybuilding competitions. Louis has won more titles than anyone else, but this fact doesn't make me feel like any less of an imposter, especially since I don't know how to lift weights and can't afford a membership or even a day pass. As if on cue, the guy at the counter stops me with one of his bulging forearms.

"You can't go in there," he says. "Members only."

"I need to talk to my brother, Louis."

He looks me over, surprised that someone so skinny and frail could be related to Louis. "He's training, dude. You shouldn't bother him."

"It'll just take a minute," I say. "It's really important."

But before he can shut me down, the most beautiful girl I've ever seen bounces up to the counter in a pink spandex tank top. She's a mess of curves, blond hair, and shining teeth. Her perfection strikes me dumb; I stand, wide-eyed, unable to think or speak.

"Hi, Trevor," she says to the guy at the counter.

"Hey, Sheila. What's up?" He gives me a nod toward the weight room, my signal to get lost.

I follow the sound of screaming death metal to the chromed, mirrored free-weight room. It's crowded, but Louis is easy to spot; he's at the squat rack with his buddies, a couple of tattooed monsters I've never seen before. A barbell rests on the back of Louis's neck. It's loaded with so many steel plates that the bar is actually bending under the weight. His face is twisted with effort, and beads of sweat line his forehead.

"You got this!" one of the monsters says as Louis sinks down into a squat.

"Push it out!" says the other. "Push it!"

Louis's quads bulge as he rises. I half expect his knees

to explode, but they don't. When he finishes his set, they all give each other high fives and shoulder bumps. One of his friends notices me and whispers something to Louis. I wave, but Louis doesn't wave back; he grabs his duffel bag and walks over, scowling.

"What are you doing here, James?" he says.

"I don't know. Nothing."

"You're supposed to meet me at five o'clock, not two."

"I know, but I thought . . ."

"What did you think, James?"

"I thought that maybe we could hang out and you could show me how to lift. You know, like we talked about."

"When did we talk about that? I don't remember."

"A little while ago. Before you moved out."

"That was, like, a year ago." He pulls a towel from his bag and wipes some of the sweat from his face and his shaved head. "Listen, James. I don't mean to be an asshole or anything, but I don't have time for this. I'll meet you at Taco Bell at five, like we planned. Okay?"

"I could just hang out and watch. I don't even have to work out or anything. I'll be quiet."

"I don't think so, James. What's up with your eye?"

"Nothing." I touch it. My fingertips explore the swollen discolored edges.

"We'll talk about that later." He taps me lightly on my shoulder and walks back to his buddies. "Five o'clock," he says. "Don't be late."

I walk with my head down past Trevor and Sheila. They're still smiling and flirting, and why shouldn't they be? They're good-looking and cool; they belong here among the weights and mirrors and the other people who are good-looking and cool. They look so happy and perfect, like they're in a movie or a music video. All that's missing is the film crew and the sound track. Out of sheer loneliness, I wish I could be just like them. If I had enough money for a gym membership, I could get buff, too. And then I wouldn't be a skinny, friendless loser anymore. Kids at school would respect me. Louis would want to hang out with me, and we'd be like real brothers again.

4

I honestly don't know what I was thinking, showing up at Dirk's in the middle of his workout. I should have known better. Ever since Louis moved out, he's wanted nothing to do with me—until yesterday, when he asked if I wanted to come work for him. He said his roommate, Vern, freaked out and joined the marines, leaving Louis shorthanded for deliveries. I don't believe this for a minute, because Vern can't get out of bed before twelve o'clock, much less march and do a thousand push-ups. But it doesn't matter. What's important is that we'll be business partners, and maybe, in time, buddies.

A dirt trail at the back of the gym parking lot leads me to the train tracks, where I can walk the rails to kill time. I go heel to toe for a hundred feet or so, until I lose my balance and fall off. The trestle is raised about ten feet, which gives me a good view of all the backyards and parking lots I pass by. At the Dunkirk Ice Cream plant, a worker in a white smock and a hairnet leans against the factory's corrugated yellow siding, smoking a cigarette. He gives me a nod, and then stubs out his butt before returning to work.

Ahead I see a bunch of kids throwing rocks at the old Brooks Locomotive Works, a low-slung brick building that stretches forever on a street that runs parallel to the tracks. The small square windowpanes are long gone; the kids chuck fist-sized trestle stones into the factory through the empty frames. They watch me carefully and, when I get too close, drop their rocks and disappear on bicycles.

I'm getting hungry and tired, so I decide to stop for a rest. I dig out my change: seven pennies, two nickels, and a quarter. It's not enough to buy anything with, so I put the coins on top of one of the rails and sit down to wait for the next train. Louis and I used to do this, up until he started high school. Those were some of the good times in our lives, before our mother fell apart and started dating Ron. We used to spend hours lining up a hundred pennies at a time on each rail. They'd stretch out forever, an endless line of gleaming copper dots. Later, after they were flattened to the size of half-dollars, Louis would sell them at school for a quarter apiece. We'd go right after to the movie theater to buy tickets, and candy, and giant buckets of buttered popcorn.

Waiting, I look at a scrim of weeds separating the trestle from the road. It has trapped all kinds of garbage: pop cans, scratch tickets, and shredded bits of newspaper; pizza boxes, empty forty-ounce bottles of malt liquor, half of a Nerf football. I sit down with my back against the telephone pole and spot a whole new cache of debris: a pretzeled bicycle wheel, half a waterlogged porno magazine, and the colored plastic shards of what might have been a squirt gun. How many kids, I wonder, have come to this place to throw rocks, watch trains, and flatten coins on the steel rails? Probably a lot.

After the train thunders by, a double-engine Union Pacific with thirty coal cars, I pick through the rocks on the trestle and find only two pennies. They're completely smooth and wafer thin, about the size of a quarter. I get back up on the rail and start walking, heel to toe, heel to toe, turning one of the big smooth pennies in my fingers. Maybe I'll give it to Louis, and he'll remember the old times when we had fun together.

5

After a few hours of walking, I meet Louis in the parking lot of Taco Bell on Bennett Road. He's waiting in his blue and white Bronco, eating a bag of burritos. The Bronco is his pride and joy. He's spent years restoring it, and it is absolutely perfect, with metallic paint, three-piece rims, and a lift kit. Not that I know anything about trucks, but Louis tells me, and I try to listen because he's smart, and tough, and good-looking, a guy who is going places. Someday I am going to look in the mirror and see someone more like him than me. Someone with cool clothes and muscles instead of ratty sweatshirts and a bony fifteen-year-old frame. Someone with confidence, and that hard look in the eyes that commands respect, maybe even a little bit of fear.

"You're late," Louis says, stuffing his mouth with the last bite, which makes me sad, because I half hoped he had bought me something. He crumples the bag and turns over the small-block eight-cylinder engine. The sound is a deep rumble that runs through my body. It makes me feel tough and invincible, which is funny, since I think of myself as being mostly weak and breakable (because I'm no good at sports, I bruise at the slightest touch, and I can't fight or stand up for myself). But it's good to drive around with my big brother, pretending to be different.

"It's five o'clock," I say, but Louis points to the digital display outside the bank, which says 5:32.

"My watch must have stopped," I say.

Louis laughs and taps the side of his head. "You don't have a watch, genius."

"Oh, right."

Louis shakes his head, like he can already tell this isn't going to work out, like he's making a mistake in asking me to help him.

He points at the remains of my black eye.

"Did Ron do that?" He clenches his fists, no doubt considering a detour to give my mother's boyfriend another ass kicking.

"I'm dealing with it." Which is a total lie, but as much as I'd like Ron to get what's coming to him, Louis's probation officer said one more assault charge against Ron and Louis'll get real prison time.

"Tell me," Louis says, scratching his square stubbly jaw.

"I have a plan."

Louis shakes his head. "No, you don't, James."

"I do!" But he's right; I have no plan. The truth is that I'm terrified of Ron, which is partly why I'm never at home. And it's why I wander around so much. Even when it's cold and I'm hungry, walking is better than getting my ass beat.

13

"You're not going to do shit, and you know it. You're just a kid."

"I'm fifteen." I know how stupid this sounds, but I don't feel like a kid, at least not like the kind of fifteen-year-old kid who should be hanging out with friends and getting busy with girls. For one thing, I don't have friends. And there have never been any girls. But the main reason I don't feel like a regular kid is because I have to worry about so many things. I worry about Louis staying under the cops' radar. I worry about my mother paying the rent on time so we won't get evicted again. I worry about what I'm going to eat next, and if I'll ever have enough money to take a girl out on a date (assuming that there will someday be a girl who would go on a date with me). But my biggest fear is that the world has made up its mind about me: I'm not wanted. I'm out. This is what fills my head when I walk the trestle that cuts through the backyards of other peoples' lives, people who are wanted. Those who fit in.

"Exactly," my brother says, like it's settled. "We'll talk about this later."

6

Louis shifts the truck into gear and peels out. We drive with the stereo blasting "Seven Nation Army" by the White Stripes, which he says is his own personal anthem and reflects his true kick-ass nature. I don't have a personal anthem, but I like Louis's, especially when a convertible full of high school girls pulls up at a red light; they smile and give us these seductive looks that drive me crazy but also make me feel like a fake, because, really, it's just the truck and the music and Louis's good looks. Without any of those things, I am just a lonely kid loping along the street with my head down. But right now things are different, because one of the girls looks right at me and blows me a kiss.

I want to freeze the moment and make it last in case I never get another one. I want to feel the impossible warmth of a kiss whispered through the air at a nowhere stoplight. I want to climb into the convertible with a drop-dead smile and say, "Just drive, damn it, because you are all so beautiful, so impossibly beautiful. And there is nothing outside this car except trouble and loneliness, and we owe it to ourselves to burn through the night with the music playing loud and your hair flying in my face like rivers of silk, until we run out of gas or explode or die of pure happiness."

But Louis barely notices the girls. He flicks a smoked-to-the-filter cigarette out the window and shakes loose one more. "How's Mom?" he says.

"Same," I say, which means that she is still sad and drunk and beaten down, a different woman entirely from the one who used to buy us Legos and Matchbox cars. Before the bartending job (and the lines of shots at closing time—Louis walking her home at two a.m., trying to keep her from lying down or passing out in the neighbors' front yards), she used to get up early and make us eggs and bacon arranged in smiley faces. She used to sew baseball patches onto our Little League jerseys. Before Ron, she used to call us her good boys and kiss our foreheads, leaving a lipstick ring.

Louis must be thinking these things, too, because the muscles in his face relax along with his attitude. He reaches across the space of the truck's cab and puts his hand on my shoulder, and I can't remember the last time someone touched me. I try not to get too sad about this. For a moment at least, Louis is my big brother, the same one who used to put pennies on the tracks and ride me home from baseball practice on the handlebars of his BMX bike and tell me that, if I closed my eyes and put both of my arms out straight, like wings, it would be like flying. "Keep them out," he'd say in that solid reassuring voice, "and you'll be king of the world."

King of the world, I say to myself now.

But just as quickly Louis changes back, the hard edges returning along with his attitude. I feel the switch even before he takes his hand off my shoulder and downshifts, making the tachometer jump from three thousand to six thousand rpm, into the red zone. He goes back to being Louis the tough guy, Louis the businessman. We stop in front of a run-down double-wide trailer on the outskirts of town. He thrusts a padded mailing envelope into my hands.

"Ready?"

I nod, even though I don't want to get out of the truck. Who am I kidding? I'm no drug dealer. I've seen the kids at school who deal drugs, and I'm not them. They've got tattoos, big gold rings, and hundred-dollar sneakers. They know how to fight, and intimidate. People are afraid of them. Nobody's going to be afraid of me. I'm sure of it.

I want to tell Louis to turn around and get on I-90 west. I want him to drive to Erie, Pennsylvania, and then Cleveland, Chicago, and whatever lies beyond. I want to drive in shifts, pushing the miles until we're so far away that neither of us recognizes the names of the places on the green metal highway signs, maybe all the way to the ocean or some big mountain range where people live in little wooden cabins and eat at the same country restaurant on Friday nights for steaks or the meatloaf special. We can share an apartment and get jobs, real jobs in factories or stores, or even mowing lawns. I wouldn't care. The important thing is that we'd be together, just Louis and me. Starting over. Like brand-new people.

But all of this is in my head, wishful thinking. I take the

package from Louis, surprised at how light it is; I wonder what's in it, if it's the crystal meth that fucks Ron up so badly and rots his teeth, or if it's just weed. But in a way I don't want to know what's inside, because it doesn't matter. Louis has never asked me to help before, and this is my big chance. I have to show him that I've got enough balls to do it. I can't screw it up by asking too many questions or getting cold feet.

He notices my hesitation. "I need your help, bro. Vern fucking enlisted. I can't do this myself."

I still don't believe that. Louis probably kicked him out for using their drugs. Or maybe he's in rehab. But again, I let it go.

"No worries," I say, opening the door and climbing down.

"Good," he says, checking his cell.

I stride across the muddy yard to the front door, where a fat guy in a NASCAR T-shirt and a camo cap is waiting. Through a mouthful of chewing tobacco he says, "Who're you?" He stands behind a ripped screen door, spitting brownish juice into a plastic Gatorade bottle.

"James," I say.

"I don't know you. Where's Vern?"

He looks mean and stupid and twitchy, but I know that Louis is in his truck watching. He won't let anything bad happen to me, and I want to do a good job for him.

"Not here," I say, trying to look unafraid. I show him the package.

"Fuck you. Tell Louis this is bullshit." He reaches

through the ripped part of the screen door and grabs the padded mailer. "Don't go nowhere," he says.

I wait, wondering if he's going to come back with a gun and blow my head off. Or maybe he won't come back at all and I'll have to go in after him. Or I'll have to return to Louis's truck empty-handed, which seems worse. But after a minute he comes back with a small envelope that he pushes through the torn-up door. I start to open the package even though I don't know how much money should be in it. But it seems like the right thing to do, check and make sure the guy isn't cheating my brother.

"Don't count it, numbnuts!" He spits into his bottle but misses; a line of brown juice hits my jeans. "Don't you know shit? Get your stupid ass in that truck and don't come back until you grow some fucking brains."

7

The next houses go easy, and I start feeling hopeful because it's not too hard a job, and I seem to be good at it, saying "hi" to fuckups and burnouts, handing out mailers, and then collecting. Maybe if I earn Vern's share of the rent, I can move in with Louis. Forget that Louis didn't take me with him after his first fight with Ron, almost two years ago. And forget that he hasn't called or spent time with me, except when he's needed help, like putting the top on his truck or hauling furniture. I can overlook all that stuff if it means getting out of my mother's place and the nauseating smell of failure, a mix of body odor, smoke, and spilled beer. The possibility of leaving fills me with hope, and I jog to the remaining houses.

After the last delivery, I wait in Louis's truck while he opens up the envelopes and counts the money. He peels off two twenties.

"This is for you," he says. "You didn't do too bad, James, but you can't take any shit from those assholes. You know what I mean?"

I nod, even though I have no idea what he means. How can I not take shit from 250-pound guys in NASCAR T-shirts? They're so much bigger and older. Plus they looked crazy, like there was something wrong with them. They talked to me through ripped screen doors and in dark piss-smelling stairwells. I ask Louis, "What do you want me to do if they don't pay?" I feel like a big pussy for asking, and I can feel the whole thing slipping away—this job, moving out of my mother's place, having my own money.

But Louis is cool about it. "You tell *me*." He flexes a bicep and points at it. "I'll deal with that shit."

We both smile. And then we drive to Dimitri's, by Lake Erie, to eat and hang out, which is something we haven't done for a long time. Eighteen months and twenty days, to be exact—since Louis moved out. I know the exact amount of time because we switched to a smaller, one-bedroom apartment "to save money." That's how come I ended up on the couch.

"Get what you want, bro," he says. "It's on me."

I order blueberry pancakes with three eggs, bacon, and hash browns. (I am practically always hungry, even though I'm skinny like you wouldn't believe.) Louis has oatmeal, coffee, and a side of ham, all of which he says are part of his bodybuilding diet.

"Louis," I say, "you think when you're done training I can start lifting weights with you?" I know it's a ridiculous question, because I hate to exercise or play sports. But I *would* like to get buff. And if I hit the weights hard enough, I can give a certain someone named Ron a real surprise the next time he gets loaded and thinks he can fuck with me.

21

"Maybe," he says. "How come?"

"To get strong."

Louis nods, stuffing half of the ham steak into his mouth. "I'll help you, little bro. A few weeks in the gym with me and no one will give you any shit. I guarantee it."

And I believe him, too, because Louis knows what he's talking about. I am going to get strong and become a real man, and then I can literally kick Ron's worthless ass out of the house and save my mother, even if she acts like she doesn't want to be saved. Is it possible to save someone who wants to go out in a blaze of cigarettes and vodka? I don't know, but I have to try.

No matter what, I'm happy to be with Louis. For a long time we sit and eat and hang out like two normal brothers. We talk about cool stuff like girls and cars and music and movies. Louis smiles when I remind him about his old BMX bike and the flying trick on the handlebars.

"King of the world," he says, a flicker of a smile spreading across his face. We sit quietly, both of us trying to see into the fog of a few good memories from before our dad left us and it all went bad. But then Louis's phone buzzes, clattering across the table, returning us both to the bright fluorescent lights of Dimitri's and the reality that I am a lost boy pretending to be a man.

"Tomorrow?" he says to me. He stands, reaching for his keys. "Same time, but don't be late."

8

In the morning my feet hit up against the arm of the living room couch. I am growing, but only in the tall skinny way. Louis is just as tall, but all muscle, like he's been forged out of a block of iron. I'm just skinny. Stretched thin.

If I don't wake up early, I have to look at Ron in his filthy undershirt and briefs. I have to listen to his garbage about how I'm stupid and lazy and it's my fault that he has no job and hates his life. And whenever he says those things, I just walk out, except that sometimes he blocks my way and shoves me and calls me a disrespectful little shit. "Look at me when I talk to you," he says. And if I do it, he slaps me so hard in my face that my eyes water. "You gonna cry?" he'll say, but it's not that. Because if you slap someone hard enough in the face, their eyes are going to water and it's not necessarily tears.

The last time this happened, which was two days ago, he said, "Don't be such a pussy, James," and then he hit me again in the same spot. My mother was in the room, getting ready for work. She stood in her barmaid's uniform with a pained look on her face, like she was torn between the two of us. Like there was any real choice between an unemployed drug addict and her youngest son.

Ron pointed at her and said, "Don't give me any shit, Doreen. I'm just trying to toughen him up." So my mom left the room and sat at the kitchen table, chain-smoking a pack of unfiltered Camels down to her nicotine-stained fingers, waiting to disappear into the bluish haze of her own recycled smoke. She looked used-up way beyond her thirty-nine years. Sad. Tired. Nothing left for anyone else. I bolted out the door, holding the side of my face, squeezing my eyes shut to stop the flow of tears. *I hate my life*, I thought. *I hate myself. When will it end?*

Louis tells me to fight back, and I think about it every day, fantasizing about how I might do it if I could become strong and unafraid, but I can't bring myself to act. It's like my cells are afraid. They shake and quiver, and then my nerves won't tell my muscles to move. But even though my mother chooses to have a boyfriend who is crazy and ugly and a loser, I don't want to cause her any more trouble. So each morning I wake up, roll my blanket, and pull on a sweatshirt and my worn-out sneakers. I walk until I am no longer angry and scared, until I don't care about the hits and insults. I pound the sidewalk, and in time, the emotion leaks out of me and I am nothing but an empty kid walking.

Today is especially cold, so I pull my hood tight around my face and walk faster. I usually wander for a couple of hours until school starts. Or I sit in the student activities center at school, reading books from Mr. Pfeffer, my English teacher. So far this year he's given me *Rule of the Bone*, which is kind of like *The Catcher in the Rye*, but only if Holden Caulfield lived in a trailer and had a Mohawk. And he gave me *I Am the Messenger*, which is about an under-age taxi driver who accidentally stops a bank robbery. I read those two books cover to cover the way my mother smokes her cigarettes, lighting new ones off the burning tip of the last, reading only to lose myself in the words and disappear.

Sometimes when I walk, I take Lake Shore Drive past Tim Hortons, wishing I had enough money for a doughnut and a mug of hot chocolate. I always brace myself against the cold wind that blows off the lake from Canada, but that never helps. Half freezing, I follow Erie's shore, which looks empty and abandoned. The lifeguard stands and overturned aluminum fishing boats have been tagged by graffiti and covered in bird shit. I walk by Pangolin Park with its empty ball fields and volleyball pits, and past streets named after strange animals: Ermine, Genet, Lemming, Jerboa, Armadillo, Serval.

Other times I go to Canadaway Creek to watch fisher-men wading into the current, slow-moving brown and green figures blending with the water, becoming a part of it. They wave their lines in circles above their heads like they're gathering forces or working magic, and I imagine that one day, when I am older, I will buy a set of waders and a fishing pole and join them. I won't even care if I catch anything; it will be enough to stand among them in the rushing water, a kind of quiet meditation to put my mind at ease and help me remember that the world isn't such a shitty place after all. Or if it is, it will remind me that I can still come here and forget that I'm hungry and have no friends.

But today is different because I have money, so I walk in a totally different direction, to Rusty's Diner for breakfast. The waitress is this pretty twenty-something-year-old with blond hair that's piled up on her head in a really nice way. She's not at all like the girls at my school with their low-cut jeans, belly button studs, and back tattoos. She looks good, though, and as crazy as it might sound, I wonder what it would be like to kiss her. She's got the beginnings of lines at the edges of her eyes, which totally disappear when she smiles, so she looks young and happy, but only when someone makes the effort to make her smile. I'm guessing this doesn't happen very often at Rusty's, because some old guy in a highway worker's uniform is already giving her a hard time.

"Do you even remember what I ordered? Because it sure as hell wasn't a Western omelet."

She apologizes and takes his plate away as a silence falls over the half-dozen tables. I want to tell that guy to shut his mouth and not talk to pretty women like that. I want to look him in the eye and make him apologize—"Now say you're sorry, asshole!" But I don't do anything, because that's movie stuff and I'm not that guy. I don't know what to say to make her smile and do that thing where her eyes light up and her face changes just because she's found a little bit of happiness in an otherwise crummy day. Still, it's good to imagine, and I get lost in a fantasy where she

26

touches my arm and says, "James, are you going to take me away from this awful life? I know I'm a little old for you, but I really think we can make it work."

Crazy, I know.

"Are you ready to order?" She's standing over me with her little pad, and I'm embarrassed because of the stupid shit I have been thinking. "Do you need some more time?" she says.

"No. I know what I want."

She taps her pad, smiling, waiting for me to find my wits and speak again.

"Bacon and eggs, please. And French toast."

"My, you must be hungry. Anything to drink?"

"Coffee. Black." I don't know why I say this, because I've never had coffee before. But all the guys at the counter have steaming mugs, and I want to look like a regular guy. She fills my cup.

"I'll get your food out in a minute, hon."

Nobody has ever called me that and it feels nice, even if she probably says it to everyone. I'd like to say something nice back to her, but nothing comes to mind. Then my food arrives and I dig in because I'm starving, and the guy next to me at the counter, an old-timer in a red plaid shirt and suspenders, slides me a bottle of ketchup and hot sauce without saying a word. I like this, too, and decide it's a sign that I belong here, that I can come back whenever Louis pays me. Maybe the waitress and I will get to know each other's names. I'd like that.

"Can I get you anything else, sweetie?" she says.

I shake my head because I'm full, and also because I

am struck dumb by the nice things she keeps saying. I know these are not romantic things, but still, it feels good. Without thinking, I blurt out, "You have really nice eyes when you smile."

She touches my arm and says, "You just made my day, sweetie. If you were ten years older, I'd tell you to pick me up after my shift."

"So what time is your shift over?" I say, wishing I could press a button and gain ten years.

She winks and glides away to the other customers. I leave a five-dollar tip and hustle out of there for fear of what other stupid things I might say.

9

At school, Earl, the morning janitor, pushes his cart slowly, humming along to the oldies songs on a small transistor radio he keeps bungeed to a mop handle. Earl looks impossibly old, too old to work, but I don't think he minds, because every time I see him, he is humming and happy to see me.

"Morning, boy," he says, shaking my hand. "You got my coffee, right? Two sugars."

I put my hands out to show that they're empty.

"All right, then," he says. "Tomorrow you owe me two coffees and . . . and one of them egg sandwiches. With cheese and bacon on it."

He laughs to let me know he's kidding, but tomorrow I *will* bring him coffee and an egg sandwich. Because I know what it's like to be hungry and thinking about what you'd like to eat. I'll surprise him, and he'll say, "What's this?" And I'll say, "It's just breakfast, Earl." And he'll say, "Naw, boy, you don't need to do that. You keep your money." But

I'll insist, and maybe he'll have a great morning because I have a job now and I can afford to buy Earl a cup of coffee.

I walk down the hallway with a dozen or so robotics club and band students hurrying to their Advanced Placement classes. They carry violin and trumpet cases, and pieces from computer circuit boards, talking excitedly about scales and concertos and bits of programming code. They laugh and slap each other's backs and stumble into each other on purpose in the way that kids are always touching each other.

I am ashamed of how badly I want what they have. Am I really that different? So different that I will have to walk these halls alone, friendless, for another two years? I wish I was good at something like sports, or an instrument, or even smoking cigarettes, which isn't really a skill or an interest but at least it's something to do, something I could have in common with other kids who smoke. If I smoked, I could go right now to the green steel bridge next to school and say to a kid sitting on the railing, "Can I bum one of those?" and they would nod ever so slightly, looking impossibly cool and aloof. And I would lean back against the railing, too, blowing out my indifference to the world in perfect smoky rings. But I can't do it, because it makes me cough like a spaz, and I don't know the first thing about being cool or aloof.

I turn away from the group of computer and band kids and go in to Mr. Pfeffer's dark empty classroom. I take a seat, suddenly exhausted even though it's only eight-thirty. Maybe it's because I am finally full and warm, and for the moment, there's nothing for me to worry about. I put my head down and close my eyes, but after what seems like only thirty seconds, Mr. Pfeffer bursts through the door with his gray-black beard and booming voice. "James," he says, flipping on the lights. "How's my favorite writer who doesn't write?"

Mr. Pfeffer insists that I am a talented writer who just hasn't realized it yet. Why he thinks this, I'll never know; I haven't done anything with my life that is worth writing about, and I haven't written a word outside of his class assignments. I told this to Mr. Pfeffer, but he waved his hand and said, "It's voice and perspective, not experience. There are plenty of books by charming bastards who can't get out of the way of their own talent. The world needs more voice and perspective. Yours will do, when you're ready."

I pick my head up, rubbing my eyes, grateful that my favorite teacher, a man I admire and look up to, likes me, even if I don't understand why.

"Here." He pulls two bottles from a mini fridge under his desk. "Have a root beer, and let's talk like real men about *The Sea Wolf*." He assigned the book by Jack London last week, daring any student to prove to him that it's not the absolute greatest American adventure novel ever written. It's about Humphrey Van Weyden, otherwise known as Hump, an intellectual and self-described sissy who gets plucked out of the sea by a sealing schooner. Van Weyden thinks he's been saved . . . until he meets the captain, a brutal madman named Wolf Larsen, who forces him to stay aboard and serve as cabin boy. I've only read a few chapters, but I can tell Van Weyden is going to have to fight Wolf Larsen for his life. It's that kind of a book, which is to say, it's awesome.

I twist off the bottle·cap. The ridges dig into my hands, and I do my best not to show that it hurts. "Do real men drink root beer, Mr. Pfeffer?"

"*I* drink root beer," he says, thumping his barrel chest with a meaty fist. "You saying I'm not a real man?"

"No, sir." I laugh.

"Good. You might pass yet. Now, about that book . . ."

I take a swig from my bottle; it's cold and delicious and wakes me right up.

"At the beginning," he says, "when Wolf Larsen tells Hump, *'You stand on dead men's legs. You've never had any of your own. You couldn't walk alone between two sunrises and hustle the meat for your belly for three meals,'* what does he mean?"

It's an easy question, a gift to get the conversation started. "That Wolf has no respect for Hump, because he doesn't do any real work. He's living off the work of others."

"Right," Mr. Pfeffer says. "But what's he *really* saying?" This is how Pfeffer works, a simple question followed by slightly tougher ones.

"That Hump's not a man."

"And how does Hump respond to the challenge?"

"He shrinks from it, because he's afraid." I open my copy and read from a spot I had underlined earlier: " *'What was I to do? To be brutally beaten, to be killed perhaps, would not help my case. I looked steadily into the cruel grey eyes. They might have been granite for all the light and warmth of a human soul they contained. One may see the soul stir in some men's eyes, but his were bleak, and cold, and grey as the sea itself.'"*

Pfeffer smiles broadly. "Ahh, well done, boy!" he says. We clink our bottles together as a couple of kids come in and loiter around their seats. Mr. Pfeffer leans in close. "But read the rest of this book carefully," he says. "It's got some good stuff in it. Secrets. Do you know what I mean?"

I shake my head, a little freaked out at the way he's staring at me, dark eyes blazing, focusing too intently, like they're trying to see into me. Maybe he's suspicious about the bruise on my face, thinking I'm getting punked in the locker room. Or maybe he knows that Ron kicks my ass.

"Listen," he says. "There are certain books that should be read at specific times in your life. I think this is the book for you."

"Okay," I say, even though I still don't understand.

Mr. Pfeffer leans in even closer, so close that I can smell his aftershave and the root beer on his breath. "There are things in this book that you need to know," he says. "Like when Hump finally stands up to Wolf Larsen—and he does finally stand up—Hump says a real man is one who is brave *and* scared. He says that heroes with no fear aren't really brave; they're just being themselves. But a scared guy being brave . . . that's the real thing." Pfeffer arches a bushy black eyebrow, which is what he does whenever he introduces a paradox, two things that should be opposites but aren't.

He lets me hang on to that point and turns his attention to the rest of the kids filtering in before the eight-fifty bell. I think about Pfeffer's paradox, hardly listening to his booming lesson just a few feet away. How is it possible to be brave *and* afraid? In my mind I run through everything I am afraid of, the awful terror I feel when Ron pokes his thick finger into my chest and says, "You think you're something special because you read them books and shit? Well, I got news for you. You ain't nothing but a . . . a trained retard, a weak sack of shit . . . an embarrassment to your mother. That's right, she cries herself to sleep at night worrying about you and your asshole delinquent brother."

I think about the kids on the lacrosse team who jump at me in the hallways with their sticks and their stupid-cool fauxhawk haircuts, only to laugh and call me a pussy when I flinch and back away. How can you not flinch when someone jabs a stick in your face and shouts at you? What are you supposed to do, stand there and take it? What would Louis do? He'd probably kick their asses and then beat them with their own sticks.

I think about all these things, and it seems impossible that I will ever become a real man. How am I supposed to learn? From the movies, or from watching other guys at school? Who's supposed to teach me? Louis is too busy, and I only see Mr. Pfeffer in class. I want so badly to be able to stand up for myself, to be a man and work, to hustle the meat for my belly, as Wolf Larsen put it. I want to protect my mother, and earn respect. And someday, I want a girl to take me seriously enough to trust me and fall in love with me.

I hope like hell Mr. Pfeffer's right, and *The Sea Wolf* is *the* book I'm supposed to read at this time in my life. And maybe if I try hard enough, if I push through my fears and don't pussy out, I can change. I close my eyes and set my jaw to look more like Louis, and I make a silent pledge: I will study this book carefully to learn what might be hidden within its pages. I will listen to Mr. Pfeffer, and to Louis. And before the end of the school year, I will stand on my own two legs. I will become a man.

10

Throughout the rest of class I stare at my paperback copy of *The Sea Wolf.* The cover shows a schooner plunging through a black sea, and I begin to doubt that the 244 pages can hold as much meaning as Mr. Pfeffer promised. How could they? Jack London is dead. And he never knew about meth freaks like Ron, and my mother's gray lifeless skin, or the way she stares out the window ignoring the calls from work: "Doreen, are you coming in to work tonight? Doreen, pick up. I know you're there. Don't flake out on us again." He never knew about the lacrosse players, either, or the suspicious way the little kids look at me, like they know I don't belong.

But I do trust Mr. Pfeffer, so after school I walk a few blocks to the creek and sit in the sun on a big flat rock. The fishermen walk by in their khaki vests and felt-soled waders, slipping quietly into the water. I open my book and read. Wolf Larsen says, "It is a whim of mine to keep you aboard this ship. . . . And keep you I will. I may make or break you. You may die today, this week, or next month. I could kill you now, with a blow of my fist, for you are a miserable weakling."

I want to read more, to find out what's going to happen to Van Weyden, but the air has started to cool, and I don't want to be late. One of the fishermen wades out of the creek, a really old guy with deep lines baked into his smiling face from the sun and wind. I ask him for the time.

"Four o'clock." He taps his watch and crunches away over the stony shore.

I get up and start walking the same route I did the day before, past the old abandoned steel mills, and then through the nicer neighborhoods bordering Fredonia, where the state college is. But this time I blow past the dandelion fluffs and the kids on their Big Wheels and scooters. I ignore the inviting houses with their blue glowing television sets inside comfy living rooms. And I think that maybe I *am* changing. Maybe I *am* growing up a little bit because I've got a job now, and a book that Mr. Pfeffer says will teach me how to be a man. I've got purpose.

I turn right onto Central Avenue and head toward the strip mall. Louis is waiting for me at the parking lot, but he's not in his Bronco. Instead he's got this crappy little Honda with holes in the door. The holes bleed lines of rust like the car is wounded and hasn't got long to live. I look inside to make sure it's him, because the Louis I know wouldn't be caught dead in a rusted Civic. But it's Louis, all right; he sticks his head out the window and calls to me.

"Get in," he says in this businesslike kind of way, without any of the "little bro" stuff from the other day. And I can tell something's wrong, because he's got a cut-up face and a busted lip. He looks like I do after a bout with Ron, but his left arm is in a sling, too, like whoever did this really took it to another level.

"Louis . . ."

He shuts me down with his good hand. "I need you to shut up and listen."

I stay quiet even though my mind is racing. Where is his Bronco? And what happened to his face? Who did that to him? A selfish part of me wonders if I'm at risk, but then I put the thought away. Louis pulls out a pack of Marlboros and shakes one loose.

"The car is temporary," he says, lighting the smoke with an unsteady hand. "I owe money to these guys, so I can't pay you today. But I'll get you back."

"What guys?"

"Just some guys."

Who would beat up Louis and take his truck? I pull out and offer him twenty-five bucks (what's left from this morning). He says, "This is bigger than twenty bucks," but takes it.

"Twenty-five," I say. "I only bought breakfast." Thinking of it reminds me of the pretty waitress, how she said she'd go out with me if I were older. I'd like to tell him about it, but I know he's not interested, which kind of makes me sad and mad at the same time. I should be able to tell him stuff about my life, shouldn't I? Why doesn't he want to know? It's what brothers are supposed to do, talk to each other.

"Whatever." He forces out a stream of smoke and takes a final drag before tossing the butt. The window won't roll back up, and he pounds on it, cursing.

"How much bigger is it?" This means that we won't be going to Dimitri's later on tonight. Louis will want to be alone to think, and then I won't have anyone to hang out with. I'll have to go home to Ron and my mother's shitty couch.

"Way bigger. You can't even comprehend."

Louis touches the side of his face that's cut up, and says, "Let's get to work." He hands me a black messenger bag filled with mailers. I'm not sure, but I think he looks scared.

"Shouldn't we let things blow over?"

But right away I see that he's not scared. Louis doesn't get scared. He gets pissed off. Pissed off because I ask too many stupid questions. Pissed off because some guys took his truck. Pissed off because his life is tough and he has to make his own money for rent and food and all of his super cool clothes. Pissed off because now he has to rely on me, and I am no one to be relied on.

His eyes are blazing, nostrils flaring. "How do you think I eat and pay rent? Don't be stupid, James. I've worked my ass off to get to this point, so just keep your mouth shut and do what I say."

What's he mean, "to this point"? Beat up and rattled in a crappy car? But I keep quiet. I sling the bag over my

39

shoulder and climb out. I don't know what trouble Louis is in, and I don't like it that he owes money to dangerous people. But he's my only big brother, and I can deliver a few stupid envelopes if it will help him out. I can do that all day long.

Before driving away, he says, "Follow the map. I'll be waiting up the street if you run into trouble."

11

The map is easy because the houses I'm supposed to deliver to have been marked in red, with arrows showing the direction to walk in. At the first house there's a college-aged guy in a ripped Fredonia State sweatshirt. His hair is stuck to the side of his head, like he spilled something on the floor and then lay down to sleep in it. "Dude," he says, "you're late. I mean, what the fuck?"

"Sorry, dude," I say.

"Don't 'Sorry, dude' *me*, asshole. I got people waiting, and you're fucking up my shit."

"I'm here now," I say, beginning to tire of delivering drugs for my brother. "You want these or not?"

He smiles, scratches his stuck-down hair, and says, "Okay. No problem. It's all good now." He takes the mailers and gives me the money.

I walk away toward the next house on the route. I give people their drugs and collect. It's easy. I wonder how much money Louis makes doing this. It must be a lot, because when he started, about two years ago, right before leaving us, he bought all kinds of expensive stuff like a fifty-inch LED TV with an Xbox, and designer clothes. But the big question is, why doesn't he make the deliveries himself? Why pay me if it's so easy? Because it probably isn't so easy. Because Louis always has his own reasons, and it wouldn't occur to him to share them with me.

Maybe it's best if I don't know . . . if I pretend to believe that Vern joined the marines and Louis is being a good brother. Just like I pretend that my mother still gives a shit about me when I leave her apartment early, when I put my head down and walk until my feet hurt and I'm hungry. A fine mist of rain coats my face and hands and hair, but I don't remember the weather changing. I don't remember seeing a cop car pull up, either, but there it is, a giant black SUV with those stealth lights on the top. I keep walking, trying to be cool . . . but inside I am freaking out. *Just act normal*, I tell myself.

Two cops with crew cuts get out of the cruiser. One has a mustache and a pink face that looks like it's been freshly scrubbed.

Oh, shit! I think. I walk by them with my head down, clutching the messenger bag against my chest with both hands. Maybe they're here for someone else.

"Hey, kid," says the cop with the mustache.

I don't stop or slow down.

"Kid, your . . . ," he says, turning with me, pointing at my feet or the ground (I'm not sure which).

Don't panic, I tell myself. But something sharp and electric is crackling through me, and I break into a sprint, feet pounding the sidewalk in wild panicked strides. I tuck the bag under my arm like it's a football and lean forward, for speed. *Run faster,* I think.

"Damn it!" he says. He's chasing me now, the sound of breathing and cop boots rebounding off the sidewalk behind me. How can he be so fast? I pump my arms to gain a little more speed, trying to close the distance to Louis, who I can see is two blocks away, waiting in his car. Something heavy hits me from behind in the small of my back; I lose my balance and sprawl onto my face, scraping my hands and forearms. I try to hang on to the bag, but it slides off my shoulder and flaps open on the cement.

My heart thumps inside the cage of my chest. I try to focus, but it's impossible. Because I've just been caught by the cops, and my messed-up, stupid life is over. In the distance, Louis's car backs into a driveway and turns around. I watch the taillights fade as he turns a corner and disappears.

12

The cop pulls my arms behind my back and slams cuffs around my wrists. Metal strikes off the bony part, but I don't say anything; I figure that getting arrested is supposed to hurt. The cop sits next to me panting, pointing at the bag.

"What's in it?" he says, reaching.

I put my cheek down on the cold sidewalk and try to get my breathing under control. *Don't go to pieces,* I tell myself.

He takes out half a dozen envelopes, all filled with twenties, and three sealed mailers stuffed with drugs. The other cop pulls up in the black SUV and leaves it running. He gets out and puts me up against the side of the cruiser, spreading my legs by tapping the insides of my feet with his boots, and then patting me down. The one who chased me reads me my rights and then stuffs me into the backseat behind a Plexiglas shield. Parked on the side of the road, they ask me about a hundred questions designed to get me to rat on Louis.

"Where'd you get the drugs?"

"I don't know," I say.

"What's your name, kid?"

"James."

"You should tell us, James. It's better that way."

"I said I don't know." It's like I'm some other person reading a script from a bad cop movie.

"Tell us who you work for."

"No one. I go to high school."

"Don't be a wiseass."

"I'm not. I was going to the creek to read a book. It's in the bag. How many drug dealers read Jack London novels?" What's ridiculous is that it's half true. I am a terrible drug dealer, maybe the worst ever. And I *do* read books by the creek. It'd be funny if it wasn't my life.

Finally the two cops give up, cursing under their breath because they think I'm a smart-ass. The one cop puts the SUV in gear and drives away. Through the back window of the cruiser I watch the mist darken the street and sidewalk. I can see the color of the grass deepening, becoming impossibly green the way it does in early spring when you've almost stopped believing that things will ever grow again. Right now it looks like each individual blade has been painted, and I wonder who will notice these things when I'm gone. Who will watch the fishermen wade silently into the deep swirling trout pools? Who will see the little kids riding their Big Wheels and playing their wild games that make sense only to them? No one, I am sure, but so what? They are stupid things to spend time thinking about anyway. If I wasn't such a loser, I would be doing more with my time, like going to parties, playing touch football in the school parking lot, or getting laid.

I touch the Plexiglas divider and pull my finger away, leaving a smudge of a print, oily circles and whorls of my sorry-ass identity. I wonder where Louis is and if he'll show up at the police station with a lawyer. There's got to be something he can do.

"Officer," I say through the hole in the divider. "What's going to happen to me?"

The driver ignores me; his partner says, "What the hell do you think is going to happen? You'll get booked and sent away for selling shit that ruins people's lives."

"Maybe their lives were ruined already." But I'm thinking about myself and not the people who buy Louis's drugs. And I know these cops don't care, because they've probably heard all kinds of sad stories, and it's no excuse.

"Shut up!" they both say.

Somehow being sent away doesn't sound so bad. Because when I really think about it, like when I'm lying on my mother's couch trying to fall asleep, or wandering without anywhere to go, or poking through the fridge hoping that something good to eat will magically appear between the half-empty ketchup bottle and the carton of spoiled milk, *staying* seems impossible. Every day there is less of my mother. The only good things have been joking around with Earl, and morning root beer talks with Mr. Pfeffer. It's not much of a life. Not really. So maybe I *should* go away.

Back on Central Avenue, I catch a glimpse of Louis's rusty car heading in the opposite direction. Leaving me. I tell myself it's not him; it's getting dark out, and there's lots of rusty Civics in town. It could be anybody. But deep in my heart I know that it *is* him, and I don't want to think about what it means.

The cop turns off Central and drives slowly, past one of the nice houses on Fairview with the playing kids. Only, the kids aren't playing anymore; they are standing on the sidewalk watching us. I raise my hand in a feeble kind of a wave, which they don't return, probably because the windows are blacked out and they can't see me.

13

At the police station more cops take my picture and type stuff into a computer. They work mechanically without energy or emotion, reading standard questions from a clipboard. Then, in a file room, a heavy guy with thick black hair and too much cologne presses the thumb and fingers of my right hand onto a black ink pad. Even his eyebrows are impossibly thick and black, and they move around when he concentrates. He takes a white note card, rolls each finger of my hand in a little box.

When he's done, he puts the cards in a file with my name on it. "You're in the system now," he says, as though this should mean something to me.

"I think I'm already in the system. I was in trouble before. A misdemeanor."

"Good for you." He takes a cloth and dips it in rubbing alcohol. "For your hands."

The small room is filled with the sound of his breathing and the smell of his cologne. It smells good, and the words *Old Spice* pop into my head, but I don't know if that's what it is. Maybe I saw a commercial for it. Maybe it's what fathers are supposed to put on before they head off to work. He looks like a father. I know he doesn't like me, but maybe he's good to his own kid. Maybe there are lots of good fathers out there, and Louis and I just got short-changed. Maybe it could have been different for us, if ours had stayed. *Fuck it,* I think. I don't need a father anyway.

The guy hands me off to a female cop, who calls home. Ron picks up on the fifth ring and shouts, "What? Who?" The cop has to hold the phone away from her ear. I can picture Ron sweaty and shirtless, unshaven, pacing the small living room where I sleep, holding a cigarette in one hand, the telephone in the other. I can almost smell the smoke and bad breath coming through the phone's mouth-piece. I hear him tell the cop that my mother doesn't want to talk to me, which I know is a lie. The lady hangs up and asks if I want her to call anyone else.

"No," I say, even though I *do* want to talk to Louis and ask him where the hell he is, and why he left me. Is he getting a lawyer? Is he picking up Mom? He's the one who could tell me what to do. He would tell me how to handle myself, what I should and shouldn't say. But I am afraid that he won't answer his phone. Or worse, he will say, "Sorry, bro. You're on your own now. Don't tell them shit about me. I don't exist to you anymore."

And I don't think I could handle that. It's such an awful thought that I decide to put it out of my mind and never think of it again. I go so far as to imagine an old-fashioned safe, the square heavy kind that they used to have in mov-ies. I put the bad thought inside (written on an imaginary piece of paper: *Louis left you . . . again!*) and slam the door shut. I spin the dial and lock the memory up for a long time.

I sit down on a hard wooden chair next to a couple of other kids in an otherwise empty room. One of the kids is crying, but when he sees me looking at him, he says, "The fuck are you looking at?"

I say nothing because I don't care about anyone else right now. He can curse or threaten me all he wants. I don't give a damn.

He says, "I'm talking to you, bitch!"

I turn away, and after a moment, he goes back to crying. A man with a badge pinned to the pocket of his suit jacket comes in and touches the cursing kid on the shoulder. "Tough or sensitive, Neil. Pick one and stick with it." The kid grumbles and looks down at his feet. He wipes at his eyes with the back of his hand.

"James," the guy says. "Come with me."

I follow him upstairs to a crowded office with brown metal desks and piles of manila folders overstuffed with papers. He takes one off the pile and says, "Only one prior? Trespassing on school property?"

I nod. "I didn't do anything wrong. I was just hanging out after school was closed."

"So how do you go from that to a goodie bag full of meth and twenty-dollar bills?"

"I don't know." And it's true, I don't.

"You're a shitty liar, James, and an even worse drug dealer. I heard you made Officer Slater go for a run today. Is that true?"

I put my head in my hands. Even as a drug dealer I am a fuckup.

"He wasn't after you, you know. He called out to tell you your shoe was untied. Why'd you run?"

"I don't know. I panicked."

"What would your brother, Louis, think about that? He wouldn't make such a stupid mistake."

"You know my brother?"

"Sure, I do. And I know you've been delivering for him."

"I haven't."

"Then, have fun in jail while Louis drives around in his super cool Bronco picking up sixteen-year-old girls at the bowling alley. What year is that truck, a seventy-one?"

"Seventy-three," I say.

"Right. Let me ask you something, James."

I do my best not to listen, because I know what he's going to ask me, and I don't want to hear it. He doesn't understand that I am trying to cover for my brother even though I'm scared to do it. I want to stand on my own legs. I'll bet this guy has never read *The Sea Wolf.* And he's certainly never been scared. Why *would* he be? He's got a gun and a badge. He's an adult.

"Would your tough-guy brother do the same for you?"

"Yes." But I know it's not true, and this fills me with sadness and shame, though I don't know why it should. I cover my eyes with the palms of my hands, trying to block out the image of my brother driving away, the red of his taillights bleeding through.

"Then where is he? All he has to do is walk in here, and

51

I'll cut you loose. I don't even want you, James. You're a little fish. You're not worth my time."

The detective guy puts his feet up on the cluttered desk and laces his hands behind his head. "I have a boy about your age. He got in trouble once. Stole a car with his idiot friends and crashed it. All of them drunk, too. I wanted to kill him, if you want to know the truth."

I pull my hands away from my face.

"What happened?"

"Nothing!" He stares at me like I'm nobody, like I'm only the thinnest, faintest image of a dumb kid. "Because I looked out for him. I helped him get out of trouble. Because that's what families do."

"Oh."

"So who's looking out for you, James?"

I turn to stone. I am listening, and I hear the words, but I don't want to think about their meaning. I see Ron with his black cracked teeth and the sour acrid smell you can only get from blowing mom's rent money on a three-day meth binge. He and his sweaty tweaker friends are partying in the living room while my mother sits at the kitchen table, vacant, as though the smoke leaking from her cigarette is the last part of her that really matters or cares, and there's nothing she or anyone else can do to stop it from dissipating, because, after all, it's only smoke. And I can see Louis, too, driving around with a bruised eye and his arm in a sling, wondering how he's going to pay off those guys and get his precious truck back. Like he cares more about the Bronco than me.

"I guess I have to look out for myself," I say.

"Do that by telling me what I want to know. That's how you look out for yourself."

"I can't. I'm sorry." And I really am, too, because I believe this guy when he says he doesn't want me. Even though I don't know his name or anything about him, I believe him. But, still, I can't do it. I can't rat out my brother.

He shakes his head in disgust. "Christ," he says. "How fucking stupid can you be? You didn't even know what you were selling, did you?"

I shake my head.

"Then I'm sorry, too. You'll spend the night here and see a judge first thing in the morning." He stands and stretches. "It's a shame you have to go down for someone else. You don't seem like such a bad kid."

14

The juvenile detention part of the county courthouse is on the third floor. It's an old brick and stone building downtown, just a few blocks from the lake. The main hallway is covered in wavy, chipped plaster that shows a dozen shades of blue, white, and off-white from decades of repainting. It smells like paint fumes and disinfectant.

After a dinner of hot dogs and macaroni and cheese (served on a cardboard tray with a flimsy plastic spork), I sleep fitfully in a small cell with bare pockmarked walls. Someone has connected the pocks with lines of permanent marker that outline a giant "Fuk You!" In the morning I wake with a start on my tiny cot, disoriented, thinking that I'm still at home on my mother's couch. Slowly I remember where I am and what has happened—making deliveries for Louis, the pretty waitress at Rusty's, getting busted.

I try to pace back and forth between the "Fuk You!" wall and the cell's door, but there's not enough space; three strides and I'm at the other side. Eventually the memories find their way in, and I sit on my cot leaning against the wall. I think back a couple weeks to a rare morning when Ron was out of the apartment and my mother wasn't sleeping off a hangover. She shuffled silently through the kitchen with her head down, ashamed of the welts and bruises dusted over with makeup. She scooped coffee grounds into the machine and then placed her thin hand over mine, letting it rest for a moment, as if to say through a single cold touch, "I love you, but I'm not strong enough to fix this."

I wish I had said something to her, something simple and half true like, "I love you, too, Mom. I understand, and it's okay." But I didn't say anything, because I don't understand. And it's not okay. Not really. So I did the only thing that made sense at the time: I pulled back my hand and walked away.

A knock on my door tells me that it's breakfast.

I sit at a table with Neil, the cursing/crying kid from the lobby. We each get two little kid-sized boxes of Corn Flakes, with milk and orange juice, and a paper plate of congealed scrambled eggs. Even though it looks awful, I'm starving, and happy to have something to eat.

"Sorry I was in your grill yesterday," Neil says, apparently no longer angry or tearful. He tugs at the collar of his shirt and scans the room nervously. "I hate this fucking place. I need a cigarette."

Neil shovels eggs while he talks. He seems calm, almost relaxed. "You going to residential?"

"I have no idea," I say.

"I been everywhere," he says with pride. "Morton's the worst. Don't get sent to Morton; they beat the living shit out of you there."

"For real?"

"It's true. My friend Octavio got his jaw busted by the guards on his first day. They fucked him up as soon as he walked in the front door."

"Why?"

"I don't know. 'Cause they can."

A guard brings us a garbage can and motions for us to dump our trays. When we're done, I shake hands with Neil and wish him good luck.

"Good luck to you, too, man," he says. "Watch yourself and don't trust no one."

15

I follow a guard downstairs to one of the courtrooms, where I stand before a gray-haired judge who looks tired and mildly disgusted, like he might have eaten some of my eggs. He glares over the rims of his glasses and says, "Criminal possession of a controlled substance with intent to distribute. Young man, are you aware of the seriousness of your charges?"

"Say, 'Yes, Your Honor,'" whispers a guy in a gray suit who says he's my court-appointed lawyer. I look at his average face and his average haircut, and I know that in a few minutes I won't be able to remember what he looks like. How can he be my lawyer when he doesn't even know my name? I don't know his name, either. "Go on, say it."

"Yes, Your Honor."

The judge considers this for a moment as he shuffles the papers in front of him. "The defendant is remanded to the custody of the Division of Youth Services for a period of twelve months. Next!"

"Twelve months?" I say to my nameless lawyer, who is already packing up his things.

"Yes. Good luck."

I've never heard of the Division of Youth Services before, but I'm pretty sure I can't do that amount of time. The eggs from breakfast rise in my throat, but I force them back down, telling myself to breathe and not lose my head. At least it's not adult prison or that place Neil talked about. Milton, I think. So I'm grateful for that. And maybe there's a way to get out early, if you behave and work hard. I resolve to work very hard.

As if on cue, a guard with a tattoo of a baby's foot on his neck shackles my wrists and ankles. He's a powerfully built guy whose muscle is turning to fat. His name badge says MR. HORVATH.

He grips my upper arm too hard and shoves me down the hall toward the parking lot, where a big black van awaits with the state emblem painted in yellow on the door. "Transport rules," he says. "One: hands at your sides at all times. Two: I'm in charge of the music, so don't even think about asking. And three: keep your mouth shut. It's a long trip, and I don't want to hear any shit from you."

I nod and climb in next to a chubby black kid wearing plastic tortoiseshell glasses and a white button-down shirt with food stains on it. There are no other kids in the van. The driver, a small pinched-face guy with short reddish hair and a beard, hands Horvath two McDonald's take-out bags and then steers the van out into traffic; Horvath digs into the first bag and shows a smile that's as big and true as any child's. He tunes the radio to a country-and-western station, moving his massive rounded shoulders to the slow, twangy beat, singing in a surprisingly clear voice: "I'm not big on social graces; Think I'll slip on down to the oasis; Oh, I've got friends in low places."

The red-haired driver laughs and taps the slow rhythm on the steering wheel. He turns off Central Avenue and heads toward the thruway tollbooth. I'm going to pay close attention to the directions so I can tell Louis. Maybe he can come visit and help the time go faster.

"What are you in for?" the other kid says.

I don't want to have a conversation with him or anyone else. I mean, I am in a van being taken to some kind of kids' prison. And I feel like I might puke or pass out. What will happen if I pass out? Will they still take me to lockup, or will I get to go to a hospital? It's an interesting idea. How sick or crazy do you have to be to go to the hospital? And do they send you home after, or back to lockup? I could think about it more if this kid would just shut up and leave me alone. "It's complicated," I mutter.

"Always is, white brother." He holds a shackled fist up for a bump. I oblige, even though my heart is pounding out its own rhythm of fear inside my chest, urging me to find a way out of this van and the mess of my life. But it's no use. For me I don't think there is a way out.

"I was delivering packages for someone."

"Oh. You mean you was *dealing.*" He says it matter-of-factly, like you'd talk about washing dishes or taking out the trash.

"Yeah, I was dealing. What about you?"

He points at his shirt. "Busted for good taste. Ain't that some shit?"

I have no idea what this means, but at least he's cheerful and friendly. How can a person be cheerful on the way to lockup? Maybe if you get locked up enough times, you get used to it.

We're heading east on I-90. Orderly rows of Fredonia grapes are giving way to the hardwood forests of Silver Creek, and the slow, muddy rivers that run through the Seneca Indian reservation. Huge billboards advertise the cheapest cigarettes in New York, by the carton! No taxes. Louis and my mother would definitely stop, but only if they carried their brands: Camel and Marlboro. Off to the left, past the westbound lanes, I see a giant wooden Indian chief with his arm outstretched. He's got to stand thirty feet tall; I point, but the kid ignores me and keeps talking. He talks all the way through Buffalo and Batavia, hardly stopping to breathe.

"You know how much good designer clothes cost?" he says.

"No." But I'm sure he will tell me about it whether I want him to or not. I lean back in the vinyl bench seat and breathe, letting the air out in a slow steady stream. And with each exhale, I lie to myself and say that everything will be okay.

"Well, I'll tell you. A Dolce and Gabbana classic suit in charcoal costs a grand and four hunnert. John Varvatos shoes, two-fitty."

Except for the stains, his clothes are nicer than mine—but not a thousand dollars nicer.

"Bullshit," I say.

"Not these. These is Old Navy. Cheap shits. But the ones I stole, they was nice."

"You got locked up for stealing clothes?"

"*Designer* clothes. Tasteless stuff like hoodies and jeans get you probation. But Dolce and Gabbana's grand larceny, baby!"

16

I look out the window at the passing trees and farms.
A little while after Rochester, we pass a sign that says
FINGER LAKES EXITS; I've never been to any of the lakes,
but I remember studying about them in earth science—six
deep finger-shaped lakes carved out by glaciers. I don't see
any water, just kids on dirt bikes and four-wheelers riding
through rows of stubbed cornfields. Other kids bounce up
and down on trampolines outside broken-down trailers.

A red barn stands with its roof torn off, showing bones
of rotted wood. I wonder if the barn will still be standing
in twelve months, when I get out, or if it will collapse into
the weeds and disappear. I wonder if I will disappear, too,
or if I will go back home at the end of my placement. But
home to what? To no friends and a brother who doesn't
care about me? To Ron and my mother in their shitty
apartment with no food and a smelly couch?

The kid next to me is *still* talking. "Hey, you been to
DYS before?"

"Where?"

"Division of Youth Services. Man, where you think we're going?"

"I don't know. Juvie, I guess."

"That's what DYS *is!*" he blurts out. "You better get with the program."

I nod, wishing I could be alone to think. But he keeps talking about clothes and all the good shops and restaurants he wants to go to in Manhattan when he's older and can move there. He sticks out his hand and says, "Name's Freddie Peach."

I shake and tell him mine.

"My man, James," he says, smiling.

Mr. Horvath, who has been devouring his last Big Mac, turns around to glare at us. He's so big and fat that his neck bulges out of his shirt collar. The baby's foot tattoo is stretched and faded, and I wonder how many more Big Macs it will take before it is unrecognizable.

"Hands at your sides!" he says. "Why are you touching him in my van, Freddie Fruit?" A glob of special sauce flies from his mouth and hits the steel cage that separates us.

Freddie scowls at the guard's wide back. "I was shaking hands."

Horvath and his friend, the driver, exchange glances and laugh. "I'll bet you were. Do it again, and I'll write your revocator ass up before we even get to the facility."

"What's a revocator?" I whisper to Freddie when Mr. Horvath returns to his country-and-western station.

"Someone who gets out and then gets busted again. You only gotta do ninety to a hundred and twenty days when you come back."

"That's it?"

"If I don't screw up, which I won't."

We ride in silence for what seems like a long time. The van turns off I-90 and heads south on Route 34 through a bunch of very small towns like Auburn, Scipio, and Genoa. There are ice cream booths and vegetable stands. I see farms with horses and Amish buggies parked in muddy front yards. Finally the van turns onto a long drive and pulls up in front of a tall fence topped with coils of razor wire.

"Is this it?" I ask Freddie, a wavy sick feeling growing in my gut.

"Yeah. This is Morton."

"Where?"

"Morton. The Thomas C. Morton Jr. Residential Center, man. Where'd you think we was headed?"

Fuck me, I think. Neil warned me: "Don't get sent to Morton; they beat the living shit out of you there."

"What's wrong?" says Freddie. "You don't look so good."

"I'm not supposed to be here."

"Damn straight," he says. "Me neither."

Mr. Horvath packs up all his fast food garbage and climbs out of the van. The sliding door bangs open, and Horvath shows his fat head, tilted, leering. "Come on out, ladies."

I try to get up, but my legs feel weak. Breakfast sloshes dangerously in my stomach. I brace myself on the edge of the vinyl bench and vomit everywhere.

17

"**M**otherfuck!" Horvath says. "Clean that shit up." He grabs a handful of napkins from the glove box and throws them at me.

I do my best to wipe up the mess, and then an electrified gate buzzes open. Freddie and I are herded through it and beyond to a series of sliding metal and glass doors. We shuffle and rattle in our leg chains, trying to keep up. Inside the building there's a big, empty waiting room surrounded by tempered glass windows.

I can see into a hallway where a line of boys stand single file dressed in khaki pants and bright red polo shirts. Some have glasses with thick black frames, and a couple of them are growing beards, half-formed patchy things that make them look sick or crazy. I don't belong here with these kids. I can't be here. They stare through the glass at Freddie and me, smirking and grinning until a guard walks by. Then they turn forward and look down at their feet, casting sideways glances.

Horvath takes off our shackles, careful not to touch

my vomit-soaked pants. "Sit down and keep your mouths shut," he says, pointing at a plastic couch along the wall.

We do as he says while he bullshits with some other guards, all big men with close haircuts and either mustaches or goatees. They talk so loud that everyone within a hundred feet can hear them go on about trucks and football teams and the size of the deer they shot during gun season. They hitch up heavy leather belts and jingle giant rings of keys. They crack jokes about each other's allegedly small dicks.

I remember again what Neil said about this place, and wonder when they will beat me. I want to be tough and unafraid, but I can't help it. I'm scared shitless of these men and what they might do to me. I watch the guards carefully, the jagged edge of panic sparking across my nerves like an electric current.

"Those two are the worst," Freddie whispers.

I ignore him and look straight ahead at the far wall.

"Horvath, he's a motherfucker. Pike, with the red beard, he's a motherfucker, too."

Horvath's eyes narrow, and he shouts across the room, "I thought I told you two to shut up!"

"Yes, sir," Freddie says. But under his breath he mutters, "Pig."

Horvath doesn't hear it, but he senses something.

"Get up!" he says.

I'm not sure if he means both of us or just Freddie. I wait for more instructions.

"I said now, puke!" I stand. He gets in my face so I can smell the Big Macs on his breath, a rotten sweet smell that brings my nausea back in sick lurching waves; I fight hard to hold it in.

One of the other guards says, "You have a problem listening to directions?"

"No. I just . . ." What do they want from me? I'm not a troublemaker. I'll follow the rules, if they'll just tell me what they are. But it's already too late. Horvath nods to the other guard, who grabs me roughly by the front of my shirt. Someone else grabs me from behind and pins my arms. I try to pull away, but they're squeezing really hard and it feels like my arms might pop out of their sockets.

I let out a scream as I'm lifted off my feet and slammed onto my face. My right cheek hits the carpet and explodes in pain. I want to touch it to feel if it's bleeding or if the skin has been rubbed off, but my arms are still pinned, and the weight of someone heavy is crushing me. I can't breathe.

"Shut up when one of us talks to you," says a voice close to my ear. "You follow orders here or you hit the floor. Understand?"

"You're hurting me," I wheeze.

The guards laugh, but I can't figure out what's funny.

"You ain't too bright, are you?" one of them says.

"Just keep your mouth shut. The more you bitch, the longer you stay down," another says.

I don't know why they are doing this to me. I kick and thrash my legs, but they push my chest and face even harder into the floor. Someone grabs my ankles, and then I can't move at all. I lie still, the sound of my ragged breath not enough to drown out the screaming in my head: *Get off me! You're killing me!*

Time passes slowly, the jackhammering of my heart lessening. The screaming in my head stops, and my muscles go slack; I feel drained, exhausted. The guards take some of the weight off me, and for a long time no one says anything. Then, as if a timer has sounded, they start to talk with each other.

"You get mandated yet?" one guard says.

"Yep. Henderson banged out sick this morning."

"He ain't sick."

"Don't care. I need the overtime. You going out tonight, Roy, or you got your kid?"

"No. The ex's lawyer says no more visitations until I go to anger management. You believe that?" It's Horvath's voice, but I can't see; he's standing outside my field of vision.

"Hah! You can go to Eboue and Samson's group. Won't cost you nothing, but you'll have to read their damn books."

"You know Roy can't read."

They all laugh. Abruptly the one on my back says, "Hey, this kid smells like puke!"

"Maybe you squeezed him too hard, Croop."

"Ah, shit," says Croop. "That's why you let me have him. You suck, Horvath!"

Horvath laughs. The weight on my back and legs is lifted, and Croop pulls me over onto my side. He says, "You stink, kid. Get up!" I rise stiffly and touch my cheek. It throbs and burns, but there's no blood.

"You're fine," he says, cuffing me on the back of my head. "But it's time to man up."

What's he mean, "man up"? I want to sit in the chair

and cover my face with the palms of my hands. I want to lie down and curl into a tight, impenetrable ball. I want my life to be over. I've had enough.

Horvath points at Freddie, who is stone-faced, sitting with his back against the wall.

"Come on," Horvath says. "We're waiting for *you,* Peach!"

Freddie stands, and the three of us walk down a long hallway lined with white cinder block walls and more tempered glass windows. Outside, on some kind of athletic field, a group of boys are gathered in a circle doing jumping jacks underneath a lead sky. Freddie tries to find me with his eyes to see if I'm okay, but I don't want to look at him. I don't want to look at *anyone,* because I'm not okay and I don't think I can pretend for much longer.

We pass heavy steel doors stenciled with the words ALPHA, DELTA, and CHARLIE. A line of boys walk in the opposite direction; they look straight ahead, like soldiers in cheap red and khaki uniforms. Horvath stops in front of the BRAVO door and taps Freddie's shoulder with the antenna of his radio.

"Just in case you forgot," he says, "*I* run Bravo Unit."

"You're senior YDC?" says Freddie.

"Shut up. I didn't ask you to talk. And it don't matter who the senior is. This is *my* unit, and everybody knows it." He leans toward Freddie, his bloated face inches away. "And I don't want any bitching from you about the food, or the clothes, or the television shows. There ain't going to be *Dancing with the Stars* or any other queer shit on the TV. We watch football or the History Channel."

Freddie scowls and moves toward the door, but the big man stays planted in his giant-sized work boots. "I'm not finished," he says. "You can be a flaming pervert on the outside, but in here you better nut up and act like you've got a fucking pair."

Freddie breathes deep and says, "No more queer shit. Got it."

"Don't curse at me, fruit. I'll write your ass up, and you can start your time with negative points. Is that what you want?"

"No," Freddie says, dropping his eyes.

"Look at me when I'm talking to you."

Slowly, painfully, Freddie looks up. His face is clenched in anger, and he holds the big guard's gaze for a long, uncomfortable moment, like it's a contest to see which of them will strike or look away first.

No one strikes. No one looks away. Horvath grunts, says, "I'll be watching you. Count on it." He shakes his ring of keys and unlocks the heavy steel door to Bravo Unit, my new home.

18

Bravo is a big open room with plastic chairs, several shelves crammed with battered paperbacks and board games, and a Ping-Pong table. Red-shirted boys play cards and watch the History Channel on a small old-fashioned television set mounted on the wall. They turn to look at me, and I don't see a single friendly face.

A black guard with a silver hoop earring and a close-trimmed beard says, "Are you James?" He is tall and thin, and his uniform looks crisp, unlike Horvath's, which is wrinkled and darkened with patches of sweat.

"Yes."

"Mr. Eboue," he says with the slightest hint of an accent I've never heard before. African, maybe, or Caribbean. He sticks out his hand for a shake. "I'll show you to your room and get you set up." He points to my cheek. "Did that happen here?"

I nod.

"You'll have to see the nurse, then. After dinner."

But I am only half listening, because I don't trust him

even though he seems nice. Because I can't trust anyone. Not the guards, not the nurse, not the other kids. Freddie could be okay, but he did nothing while the guards beat me up. He watched.

I check out my new room, number fifteen, which is walled with more white-painted cinder blocks. It's got one narrow window looking out on the barbed-wire fence and parking lot. An empty fiberboard dresser. A cot with one pillow and a thin blue blanket.

"You can clean up and relax," he says, "but don't close your door until bedtime. Any questions?"

I turn away and lie facedown on my bed, trying not to cry. *Don't fucking cry*, I tell myself, but it's hard, because whatever it is I'm supposed to do at this place, I am pretty sure I can't do it. I can't "man up" or fit in with kids who are real criminals and gangbangers. What was I thinking, delivering drugs for Louis? What was he thinking when he asked me?

I am a loser. I am scared and weak. I want to call Mr. Pfeffer and ask him what I'm supposed to do. I want to talk to him over cold root beers, and have him tell me that everything will be okay. I want him to give me new books, enough to last twelve months, so I can disappear into the pages and not have to deal with this place. I could read one book after the other, stopping only to eat, sleep, and do school or chores or whatever it is they do here. And I won't have to talk to anyone, except for Freddie or Mr. Eboue. That would be a good plan.

At some point I fall into a dreamless sleep, and it's Mr.

Eboue's voice that wakes me. "Listen up!" he says. "Chow time. Regular order. Freddie and James, I want you two at the end with me. Tight formation, everyone."

I get in line behind Freddie, squaring my shoulders like the others. We walk in single file to the cafeteria and sit at other round plastic tables bolted to the floor. My table gets called first to wait in line with Styrofoam plates at a stainless steel counter; kitchen boys in latex gloves and hairnets load us up with meatloaf, mashed potatoes and gravy, peas, and buttered bread. I am allowed two milks, two cups of water, and a bowl of chocolate pudding for dessert. It looks like school lunch food only worse, but the other boys don't seem to notice or care. They dig in and work their mouths silently. Mr. E sits down next to me at my table.

"Family visits are allowed every Wednesday between four-thirty and six," he says. "But we need a three-day notice. You have family to come visit you, James?"

"I'm not sure," I say.

The other boys at the table are looking down at their plates, eating slowly. But they're also listening. I hear whispered comments: "That boy mad skinny." "He looks like he about to cry." "Smells like puke." Mr. E shoots the boys a glance and then pats me on the shoulder.

"Then you have to be extra strong," he says. "I don't have much family, either, and it's tough sometimes." He gets up and goes over to a table that's getting loud. Almost instantly the boys seated across from me look up from their food and glare.

A Hispanic kid with an Afro says, "Where you from,

white boy?" He smiles, almost friendly, like he knows he can kick my ass if he wants to but understands it's not necessary because I'm no threat.

"Dunkirk," I say. "You?"

"Brooklyn, man. We all from Brooklyn or the Bronx."

The others nod and smile with what looks like pride.

"Where the fuck is Dunkirk?" says a small white kid with big ears and spiky blond hair. His eyes are swirling with the same manic energy that Ron has when he's tweaking on meth.

"About forty miles southwest of Buffalo," I say. "It's on Lake Erie."

"I like Buffalo wings," says a tall kid with the beginnings of a mustache. He looks a little dopey.

"Buffalo's a shit hole, ain't it?" says the kid with spiky hair. He shifts and bounces in his seat like he's wired up to springs.

The Hispanic kid looks at him and says, "Yo, Weasel, how come you're always saying other people live in a shit hole? Because your narrow white ass got 'retarded inbred trailer park' written all over it!"

Other boys laugh and say stuff like "Yo, that's fucked up," and "Weasel's mad inbred."

Weasel's eyes get big and even more crazy-looking. "I dare you to say that again, Tony. You half-breed motherfucker! I mean, where'd you get that gay-ass seventies 'fro? Because I heard your mother was bald-headed. I heard she was a one-legged whore who was bald-headed. I heard . . ."

He's rolling, like he's preaching a foul sermon in some kind of an ADHD-induced frenzy. I have seen kids like him at school, kids who are mental and hyper, but he's in a league of his own. It's funny but a little scary, too, because I don't know how far he'll go and what the other boy (or the guards) will do. If they mess you up for walking in the front door, then what will they do for this?

Tony is gripping the edge of the table, veins and cords of muscle standing out on his forearms. He looks like he's going to jump across the table and choke the shit out of Weasel.

But Mr. E stops it from going any further by grabbing Weasel and pulling him off his stool. At the same time he locks eyes with Tony and says, "You're too smart to let him run you with his mouth. Right?"

Tony nods and, almost at once, lets his shoulders drop. But Weasel keeps struggling in Mr. E's grip, shouting and talking more trash. "He started it! Get your hands off me. I can walk."

Horvath is nearby, watching, waiting, shifting nervously in his big work boots, ready for action. His face is red and puffy, and he looks like he wants to crush Weasel and then throw him around like a spiky-haired rag doll. I can picture it, but it's not at all funny, because I know exactly how it would feel.

But Mr. E says, "I got this, Mr. Horvath." He puts his hand on the small boy's neck and says, "Okay, Bobby. Show me how you can do the right thing."

Bobby, or Weasel (or whoever he is), nods, finally settling down, and they walk past a hulking Horvath, who looks angry and cheated.

19

After dinner the other boys go back to the unit; Mr. Horvath takes me to see the nurse. He points to a yellow-taped line on the hallway floor.

"Always walk on the right," he says. "Or you'll get written up. Understand?"

"Yes," I say.

The clinic is a bunch of offices and small rooms separated from the rest of the facility by another set of heavy locked doors. A guard sits outside one of the rooms in a plastic chair reading a magazine, while a boy presses his face to the small inset window to watch me as I walk by.

"Sit down!" The guard bangs the door; the boy grins and disappears from view.

I follow Horvath to an office with a stainless steel examination table. It looks like the kind of place where they put dogs and cats to sleep. He drops heavily into a chair and grabs a bowl of chocolates off a white Formica desk.

"Tired, Mr. Horvath?" says a small woman in white scrubs with purple reading glasses hanging from her neck by a cord. She pours coffee into a Styrofoam cup and hands it to the guard.

"Thanks, Terry. Three mandates this week."

"And it's only Tuesday! You poor thing." She picks up a clipboard and gestures for me to get up on the exam table. "What are we doing here, Roy?"

"Post-restraint. New kid. Puked in the van."

"Oh, my," she says, turning my head to look at my cheek. "Things aren't going well for you, young man, are they?"

I shake my head, ready to be comforted by this nice gray-haired nurse.

"Don't let Mr. Innocent fool you," says Horvath. "He's already thick as thieves with Freddie Peach."

She scowls at me like I've done something wrong, says, "I *heard* Freddie's back. Can't say I'm surprised, though. A born con artist, that one."

They go on talking like this for several minutes, like I am no longer there. Terry says that Freddie filed thirty-something grievances last year, all of them rejected.

Horvath grunts and shakes his head. "That's because he's a pathological liar."

The nurse takes a picture of my cheek, which is red and puffy like a scraped knee or a rug burn, which I suppose is all it is. The camera is an old-fashioned Polaroid; the flash pops, and the camera spits out a square of film that Terry shakes and puts into my file.

"Do you know why you were restrained?" she says, a ballpoint pen poised over her clipboard.

"No," I say.

77

Her glasses drop to the tip of her nose. She looks really pissed now, no longer a nice gray-haired nurse. Horvath stops devouring the bowl of Hershey's Kisses and Reese's Peanut Butter Cups. He's rolled the foil wrappers of the dead chocolates into tiny balls and lined them up in a neat row. "He knows why," he says. "He's just being a smart-ass."

The nurse frowns. "Okay, then. I'll ask once more. Why were you restrained?"

"I don't know."

Horvath erupts, scattering the foil balls across the clean white desktop. "That's a bunch of crap!" he says. "He wasn't following directives. That's why."

The nurse marks something on her form and says, "Not following directives. Okay, next question: Were you injured during this restraint?"

I point to my cheek.

She puckers her mouth. "Last question: Do you feel that the restraint was conducted properly?"

"I don't know."

"You don't know?" She sets the clipboard down, staring hard at me, clearly angry.

"I've never been restrained before. I don't know how it's supposed to be done."

She seems to relax a little. "So you're not aware of anything unusual about the restraint procedure that Mr. Horvath and Mr. Pike used this morning?"

"I guess not," I say, except for the madness of grown men in prison guard uniforms pinning kids' arms behind their backs and throwing them down on the ground. I don't know how it's okay, and I don't know why she needs to ask me these questions if she doesn't like my answers. I don't give a damn about any of it.

Nurse Terry picks up her clipboard and puts another mark on her form, says, "Mr. Horvath, are you ready?"

He unfolds a yellow piece of paper, smoothing it out with heavy brutal hands that look like they're better suited for working a sledgehammer on a demolition crew than filling out forms. He fists a ballpoint pen like a husky kid with a crayon and says, "Now you get to tell your side of the story. But make it quick."

From the way he keeps smoothing out his yellow form, it must be some kind of paperwork requirement. Otherwise, I'm sure, he wouldn't be asking me anything.

"I don't have a side to the story," I say.

He gathers the little foil balls and lines them up again. After a moment he says, "Then listen better from now on. I tell you to do something, you do it. Okay?"

I nod.

He unfists the pen, beckons me over with one of his big hands. "Sign on that line."

I do as he says to show I agree that I was restrained properly. I wonder what happens if you refuse to sign. They probably flatten you again.

20

Everything in Morton runs on a schedule that I'll have to memorize. For now, Freddie tells me we've got an hour of leisure or room time before bed. At eight-thirty, he says, we'll get fifteen minutes for hygiene, which is washing your face, brushing your teeth, and using the toilet. If I have to piss in the middle of the night, I've got to knock on the door to get the guards' attention so they can unlock my room. And if they don't like me, they'll just pretend that they don't hear, and it will be a long night.

Mr. Eboue gives Freddie and me each a laundry basket filled with clothes. We have to count out each item and then sign a form.

"I'm sorry you got dropped earlier," Freddie says. "I thought they'd leave you alone 'cause you don't talk junk like most kids."

My laundry basket contains a pair of red sweats, four red polo shirts, five pairs of white starchy boxer shorts, two khaki pants, and five pairs of tube socks. I also get two towels and a little metal basket with state-issued soap, sham-poo, and toothpaste.

"It's okay," I say, which isn't true at all, but I don't want to talk about it right now. How many times am I going to have to repeat that lie? Probably a lot.

Freddie points to my shower basket. "When you earn privileges, you can get real soap and shit from the commissary," he says.

"This stuff's fine."

"Suit yourself, man. You go ahead and be dried out." He picks up his stack of clothes and disappears into his room.

The Hispanic kid, Tony, calls me over to one of the tables. "Hey, Dunkirk. Sit down and play cards with me."

"What game?"

"Don't matter. I wanna talk with you. James, right?"

"Yeah."

Tony looks at me while the cards riffle through his hands like magic. "I'm only gonna say this once, so listen."

I stare back, waiting for the threat, wondering how I will deal with it. I've never won a fight before, and I don't know any good comebacks or things to say about other kids' mothers.

But Tony doesn't threaten me. "You got to look out for yourself in here," he says. "It's okay to have friends on the outside, but not in here. Got it?"

"I don't have any friends."

He deals out five cards so smoothly that they seem to float across the table.

81

"Maybe, but I see you and Freddie *startin'* to be friends. And you should second-guess that shit, James. Not because Freddie's queer. My uncle Juan is queer, and he's the best dude I know."

I pick up my cards and look at them. I have a pair of aces and a six of hearts. "Freddie's queer?" I didn't know.

Tony laughs so hard that everyone on the unit looks at us.

"You're funny, James. I like that. But it's no bullshit. Freddie's got to make his own way in here, whatever that means for him. This is his second time, so he's a revocator, which is good for him, 'cause it means he might only have to do, like, three or four months. But guys like Horvath and Pike and Crupier gonna be all over him."

"Why?"

"Five card draw," Tony says. "How many you want?"

I discard and take two.

"Think about it, man. He's a black kid from Harlem, he's a criminal, *and* he's homo. In their eyes, ain't nothin' worse. Three strikes, bro. They'll be dreamin' of ways to mess him up. When it goes down—and mark my words, it will go down—you got to stay out of it no matter what. You hear me?"

"Yeah, but why are you looking out for me?" I lay my cards out to show a full house, aces high.

"Check you out, man!" Tony throws down two pairs. He's surprised that I know how to play.

"My older brother, Louis, taught me."

"Well, you lucky, man. I got five sisters. Believe that

shit? Anyway, I'm not looking out for nobody. Just giving a little free advice is all."

A pasty overweight kid with a shaved head and weird blue eyes is sitting by himself reading from a Dr. Seuss book. He flips the pages back and forth, like he's reading at random.

"That's Oskar," says Tony. "He loves them books. *The Lorax, Horton Hears a Who!, Yertle the Turtle,* crazy shit like that."

"What's wrong with him?" I whisper.

"You ain't gotta be so quiet, man; he don't give a fuck what you say. Oskar's on, like, six or seven different meds. All he does is read them books, bite his fingernails, and sleep. Ain't that right, Oskar?"

The kid looks up from *The Lorax* and raises a hand in a sort of wave/salute. Tony and I wave/salute back.

Lights-out is at nine o'clock. Mr. E says good night to all of us, making his way around to the rooms to shake hands and shut our doors.

When he gets to me, he says, "You doing okay?"

"Yes," I say.

"I seen you talking to Tony. He's a hard worker. Follow his lead and you'll do fine. Get some sleep now."

He shuts my door and engages the automatic lock with a loud click. At first it's weird; I wonder what happens if there's a fire or a tornado or something. But it's also the first time I've had my own bedroom. And as small as it is, it's mine. No more couch, and no more Ron, at least for the next twelve months. I lie down on the bed and close my eyes without taking off my clothes or peeling back the thin blanket. Except for the distant sounds of Mr. E and another guard talking in the staff office, it is nice and quiet, and I drift off to sleep.

21

Someone knocks three times on the wall and calls my name; I look around for a speaker or an intercom, but I see nothing, just a dark room.

"Hey, man, it's me. Freddie. Talk into the vents in the heater panel."

I put my face up against the sheet metal. "Can you hear me?"

"I hear you. What did Tony want?"

I don't know what to say. I can either lie or hurt his feelings.

"He said to toughen up and look out for myself."

Freddie is quiet, thinking. "It's good advice, but Tony's different. He don't need anyone to cover his back."

"Then how come he's here?"

"Same old: running the streets, bangin', dealing weed. Plus his family's shit."

"How do you know about that?"

"You locked up with the same assholes day after day, you learn more than you want to know about them."

"How about the loudmouth from the cafeteria?"

"Bobby the Weasel? Harmless. Got the name because he stole an albino ferret—his school's mascot. That simple bastard didn't think he'd get caught! How many albino ferret mascots you ever seen?"

"None." I laugh a little, just to be polite. "I gotta get some sleep, Freddie."

"Okay."

But when I get into bed, he says, "Hey, man. Did Tony say anything else? Anything 'bout me?"

I remember Tony's words exactly and decide to listen to them. I'm going to worry about myself and do my placement as quickly as I can. If things go bad for Freddie like Tony predicted, he will have to be on his own.

"Did he tell you *what* I am?"

Damn, I say to myself. I get up from my bed and go back to sitting next to the heater panel. "Yeah, he told me."

"Well, it's true. I'm gay."

Time passes. I sit on my side of the wall waiting. For what? Am I supposed to say I don't care that he's gay? But I just don't have it in me to worry about someone else's problems. I want to worry about myself. Why can't I do that? Why can't he leave me alone?

"But so fucking what?" he says. "Freddie Peach don't need nothing from nobody. So fuck all y'all!"

I still don't want to talk, but my mouth opens. "I don't care if you're gay," I say. "But I've never been locked up, and I haven't had many friends. So cut me some slack, okay?"

The clock ticks away outside my room; it must be mounted on the wall next to my door, to be so loud.

"No friends?" says Freddie.

"Nah."

"Damn! *Sorry-ass* white boy. You worse off than my gay Negro self."

"Good night, Freddie."

"Good night, James. And hey . . ."

"What?"

"Thanks for . . . you know, for being my friend."

22

I'm trying to remember the daily schedule, which is posted on the wall outside the staff office. It never changes except for on weekends when we have leisure and rec in place of school. Here's what our days look like:

6:30 a.m.	WAKE UP/ROOM COUNT
6:45 a.m.	HYGIENE
7:15 a.m.	BREAKFAST/COUNT
8:00 a.m.	CHORES
8:30 a.m.	SCHOOL
11:30 a.m.	LUNCH/COUNT
12:30 p.m.	SCHOOL
3:00 p.m.	GROUP
4:00 p.m.	HOMEWORK/LEISURE
5:00 p.m.	DINNER/COUNT
6:00 p.m.	CLEANUP/CHORES
6:30 p.m.	LEISURE
8:30 p.m.	WASHUP
9:00 p.m.	LIGHTS-OUT/COUNT

Every time we change activities, we have to line up by the door and get counted. It seems like we're always waiting to be counted, which makes no sense to me, since all the doors are locked and there are guards everywhere. We must spend two hours per day just standing in line getting counted. The guards will call in our number on their radios:

"Two staff and eighteen residents going from Bravo to the cafeteria. Over."

Central Services, which is kind of like a control booth where they keep track of each unit's movement, will check the count and give us the green light.

"Bravo, this is Central. You have permission to move."

Like that. It takes forever, and several of the kids get screamed at because they can't stand still or keep quiet.

As far as school goes, it sucks and is insanely boring. The actual work has got to be on a fifth- or sixth-grade level, but only Tony, Freddie, and I are able to keep up. The rest tap on their desks and fidget, or else sleep. We aren't allowed to look at each other, either, which means that the guards have to sit with us and constantly yell.

"Eyes ahead, Antwon," they say. And, "Stop drumming on the table, Bobby. This ain't music class."

Weasel scowls and puts his head down.

The English teacher, Ms. Bonetta, is this very pretty dark-haired woman who dresses like she's going to work in a fancy office or something. I'm talking pearls, heels, the works. She's nice, too. We spend the class doing a writing assignment about the last book we read. I pick *Rule of the Bone*, by Russell Banks, which is one of my favorites and was given to me by Mr. Pfeffer. I write about how the main character, Chappie Dorset, is a lot like me. Because even though Chappie gets in trouble, drops out of school, and sells drugs, he is still basically a good person. At least, that's the argument I try to make in the essay.

At shift change (three o'clock), Mr. Eboue and another guard I've never seen before come in and get us ready for group. The other guard's name is Mr. Samson, and he's an absolute giant of a man. His shoulders are so broad and thickly muscled that he looks like he could be in the WWF. He's so big that he dwarfs Horvath and my brother. The boys of Bravo Unit, seated in a crooked row of plastic chairs, grin and put out their palms for Mr. Samson to slap.

He walks down the line giving us high fives and bumps, saying, "Hey," and "How's it going, my man?"

Bobby the Weasel shouts, "Do the thing!" as he bounces up and down in his chair again like he's on springs. "Come on, just once!"

Mr. Samson looks at Mr. E, who shrugs. The rest of the boys join in, "Yeah, Samson. Come on!"

He drops his hands by his belt so that one is gripping the other. He flexes his pec muscles, making them jump up and down. It's funny to watch, like his stretched-tight shirt is dancing; we all laugh and cheer. Then he takes a step toward me.

"I haven't met you yet," he says, sticking out his hand.

I brace myself for a bone-crushing shake, like Louis's, but his grip is light, almost gentle.

"I work three to eleven with my friend Mr. E," he says. "We do group every day at three with Bravo. Anger Replacement, Beat the Streets, and others. You should partic-ipate in every group, but today you can just listen. Okay?"

"Okay," I say.

"We're still working on being able to tolerate things that are unfair. Who wants to start us off?" he says, standing in front of us.

Everybody looks at their feet.

"Come on, now. Who used their skills this past week? Who had to deal with something that wasn't fair?"

Tony raises his hand and says, "I got pissed off in class and didn't do nothing about it, even though I really wanted to."

"Good, Tony. What was the situation?"

"Mr. Goldschmidt told me to do, like, a hundred math problems, and I told him I shouldn't have to because I already passed the GED and I'm leaving soon anyway. But he said it don't matter, that a GED's no accomplishment. It just means I don't have the discipline to get a real di-ploma."

Samson sighs as he considers this, his massive shoulders rising and falling with the gesture of disappointment. He doesn't say anything bad about Mr. Goldschmidt, but it's clear he doesn't agree.

"What did it feel like when he told you that?" he says.

"Man, to be honest, it felt like I wanted to get violent, you know what I mean? Like I wanted to . . ."

Samson cuts him off with a raised hand, but not before several others put in their two cents. Antwon, a lanky kid with heavy-lidded eyes, sucks his teeth and says he hates Mr. Goldschmidt. Double X, whose real name is Xavier

Xavier, says he hates all the teachers except Ms. Bonetta, who he says is fine. There are even louder murmurs of agreement.

"And what did you do about it, Tony?" Samson says.

"Nothin'. I mean, I argued a little bit to let him know it was stupid. But I did the math problems. They was easy anyway."

"And what happened?"

"What do you mean?"

"When you didn't react, when you let it go. Did anything bad happen?"

"No."

"Did you feel like less of a man?"

"No way."

"That shows you're ready to go home, Tony. Nice job."

He grins, laughing it off when the other kids call him a brownnoser.

Mr. E cuts in and says, "If you guys don't learn to deal with unfairness, your anger will short-circuit your brain and you'll get arrested, beat up, or shot. Those are the only choices."

Coty, a country kid who draws pictures of four-wheelers and NASCAR racing scenes, raises his hand. "Is that why I black out when I fight, because my brain short-circuits?"

"Could be."

Other boys say that they black out, too. Double X says he once had an argument with a friend, and then an hour later he "woke up" in a police cruiser. His friend went to the hospital with a broken nose and a dislocated jaw.

"Now I'm locked up and we ain't friends no more," he says.

"How come we're short-circuited?" asks Freddie.

"I don't know, man," Mr. E says sympathetically. "Could be lots of reasons."

"Come on, Mr. E. Tell us," Freddie says.

"Well, some of our mommas drank or did drugs when they were pregnant with us. Some of us got beat too much." He points a finger at himself to let us know that that happened to him. "You might have to talk to Dr. Souza to figure it out for sure, but I'm glad you're asking, Freddie. And I'm glad you're thinking."

Strangely, no one has anything more to say. There are no jokes or put-downs. Just a long, thoughtful silence. I look around at the other boys and try to imagine what it's like for them at home. Do they have fucked-up mothers and disappeared fathers?

Finally Mr. E says, "Good job, all of you, for acting like strong young men instead of thugs and punks. I believe in you guys, even if you're a pain in my ass and give me gray hairs in my otherwise perfect Afro. Now let's change up and have an extra half hour of rec before dinner."

It feels good to hear these words, even if I haven't done anything and we're not even close to being men. Even if we are screwups, losers, and criminals, it's still nice to hear someone like Mr. E tell us different.

23

On my second day, which is a Wednesday, Bobby the Weasel gets a visit from his father, who owns a bakery. Freddie says the man hasn't missed a week and always brings trays of pastries, enough for everyone. Today he's got brownies and cinnamon rolls. They smell terrific, and I can hardly wait to get one.

I watch Bobby and his father in the staff office, playing Uno and laughing. They eat giant sticky rolls, stuffing their faces and licking their fingers. Secretly I think that the rest of us are jealous. I know I am. Bobby's father doesn't look rich or tough or cool. He doesn't have a big-shot job or good clothes. But he seems like a really nice guy who loves his son.

It makes me wonder what that feels like, and if my father ever loved me. I think he did, because of the presents he used to bring home. And I remember once he took me fishing and it was great, even though we didn't catch anything. But then, why did he leave? Even if he didn't want to be with my mother anymore, couldn't he have stuck around for Louis and me? I was only five years old, and maybe I *needed* a father. Did he ever think of that? And maybe my mother needed him, too, judging from how she acted after he left (staying in her bedroom with the lights out, quietly crying).

Even if he couldn't stick around, he could have called or written to tell us where he was living. Something. Anything. One thing's certain: if he ever does come back, I'll be ready. I won't waste any time being mad or asking for explanations. I'll just say, "I sure missed you. Let's get to know each other."

At the end of Bobby's visit, he and his father come into the activity room, where the rest of us are sitting around, doing homework and reading books.

"Be good, okay?" says his father.

"I will," says Bobby. "I promise."

He manages to keep the promise through the next day. He even gets some schoolwork done, which surprises the teachers and the guards, who are used to nagging him constantly and asking the nurse if she can give Bobby more Ritalin. Pike gives a rare compliment, asking Bobby if he's been possessed by a smart, focused demon who might be on the road to earning privileges. Even Bobby laughs, but by the end of tech class, he looks exhausted from the effort. He closes his textbook and puts his head down, humming "Old MacDonald."

Mr. Goldschmidt, a short dumpy guy who wears one of those Amish beards, stops in the middle of a lecture about shop safety. (He teaches math *and* wood shop.) "Quit humming, Bobby," he says, which only makes Bobby do it louder.

Goldschmidt tries again. "You're disturbing my class, young man."

Crupier, aka Croop, a fairly new guard who tries to impress Horvath and Pike by being an asshole (says Tony), lets out a big sigh and hitches up his black leather belt. He walks over to Bobby real slow, boots clicking the concrete floor. Rapping his knuckles on Bobby's desk, he says, "Since you missed Mr. Goldschmidt's lesson, you can write an essay on shop safety. Go on, pick up your pencil."

Tony and Freddie sigh, like they both know where this is going.

"Make me," says Bobby without looking up.

Everyone except Crupier and Mr. Goldschmidt laughs. Crupier's face turns red. "Hey, big mouth!" he says. "Do what I say and start writing."

Bobby lifts his head up and glares at him. His eyes start to swirl with the berserk energy that might hold the secret to his ability to curse everyone out in such spectacular ways.

"Why?" he says. "Why should I do what you say? You ain't my father. I don't even listen to my father, and he's a good man. He gets up early and bakes shit for all of you fuckers so you'll treat me better, even if I'm mad hyper and can't learn for shit."

But Crupier isn't listening. He grabs Bobby's arm. "I told you to write that paper," he says, trying to push Bobby's pencil into his hand, but Bobby closes his small fingers into a tight ball.

"I said I ain't writing shit!"

Crupier's had enough. He hooks the boy's arms and yanks him out of his desk. Then Pike jumps in, and they all go down to the floor.

"Get off me!" Bobby yells. "Get the fuck off me!"

His small body bucks and thrashes to get out from under the guards. The struggle lasts for what seems like several minutes, and I don't know what to do. I look to the other kids for help, but they don't seem to know what to do, either, except shift around in their seats clenching their own fists.

Goldschmidt, who started it all, pretends like nothing is happening. "Class is still going on," he says. "You should be doing your assignment." The *assignment* is a stupid photocopied picture of a table saw. We're supposed to label the names of the different parts, like the fence, and the blade guard, and the arbor.

"Hey, mister," says Wilfred, a tall kid with a wispy mustache and giant hands. "Is this a table saw or a band saw?"

Bobby's screaming is so loud. It fills the room. It pierces my ears and gets deep inside my head until it's all I can hear, all I can think about. And still we sit at our desks, watching, consumed by what's happening to this small and mildly annoying boy with a big mouth.

"Shut your mouth!" says Crupier. "If you know what's good for you, you'll shut your damn mouth."

But there's no stopping Bobby the Weasel's mouth. He curses and makes threats like he's breathing air, even with a guard on top of him. "You think you're so tough, but you ain't tough. You're a bunch of pussies beating up on a little kid to feel like big men. Why don't you go to the gym and pump each other? I'll bet that's what you really want to do."

Laughter spreads from desk to desk until we're all cracking up. Even Oskar, the spaced-out Dr. Seuss kid, laughs. We start cheering Bobby the Weasel, because he's become a small hero, fighting for all of us with his inspired curses.

"Shut up!" Crupier says, a vein throbbing on the side of his head, tempting to explode. I wish it would, because I know something bad is going to happen and there's nothing any of us can do to stop it. We sit at our desks and watch.

"Make me, bitch!" Bobby says. "I'll do this all day long. It ain't nothing to me."

And for a second I think maybe Bobby is right, and no one can shut him up. Maybe he can take everything Crupier has to dish out. And if he can do that, then maybe I can take my time at Morton.

Crupier cranks Bobby's arms even harder so they stick out behind him, looking all disconnected and jerky, puppetlike. It'd be funny if it wasn't so grotesque, this small, foulmouthed marionette being jerked around by big men in gray and black uniforms.

Then there's a crack. It's so distinct—the Morton equivalent of a stick breaking over someone's knee. Bobby opens his big mouth and lets out the most piercing animal scream I've ever heard. I look at Tony, who is tapping his desk repeatedly with his balled-up fist. He refuses to meet my eyes. Freddie, too, avoids my gaze and instead focuses on the graffiti carved into his desktop.

Out of the corner of my eye I see Oskar, whose desk is behind Freddie's. He's standing up, chewing madly on his ragged fingernails. He takes his hand out of his mouth and points at the tangle of Bobby and the two guards. In a soft monotone, almost a whisper, he says, "Stop." And then, just as abruptly, he sits back in his chair and resumes chewing his nails.

Pike hits Crupier's shoulder and says, "Hey, Croop, man, let go. I think you broke his fucking arm."

Crupier examines the weird bend in Bobby's arm. Then he picks up his radio like it's some kind of strange object put there by someone else, and pushes the pin, which is what the guards call the small orange emergency button. Freddie says that if you push the pin, a bunch of guards will come running and clean house. Pike gets off Bobby's legs and helps him sit up.

"You broke my arm," Bobby sobs. "And I ain't done nothing except talk trash."

Then he looks down at his bent, hanging limb, and gags like he is going to throw up all over the front of his bright red polo shirt. A troop of guards arrive and take him away.

24

At night Freddie knocks three times on the heater vent. "Hey, man, how come you're so quiet?"

"Thinking about Bobby."

"Yeah, that shit's fucked up."

"They can break someone's arm like that?"

"They *did*, didn't they?"

"Yeah."

"Well, there you go."

It's hard to believe I'm in a place where kids get their bones broken by adults in uniforms. I want to go home. Even if home is a place where I sleep on the couch and pretend not to hear the sounds of Ron doing sick shit to my mother behind their bedroom door. Even if home is a place with an older brother I can't trust.

Freddie is still talking. "Bobby's got to go to another unit now."

"Why?"

"'Cause Crupier can't be around him until he's cleared for child abuse," he says.

"You mean Crupier won't get fired?"

Freddie laughs. "Hell, no, he ain't gonna get fired. They gotta do an investigation any time a kid gets hurt. But Morton investigates itself. And nobody wants to work here, so they always short staff, which is why they gonna write up a report to say that Bobby was fightin' and broke his own arm."

I don't want to talk about Morton anymore, so I ask Freddie to change the subject.

"What do you want to talk about?" he says.

"Anything. What kind of stuff do you do at home?"

"I like to dress up and go shoplifting in Manhattan. SoHo and the Upper East Side."

"What?"

"You heard me. That's where the best stores are. Bloomingdale's and Barneys. Shit like that."

"Why get dressed up?"

"Because people treat you different when you look sharp," he says. "Most of the fools in here dress like thugs. Wearing they colors and shit. And they wonder why cops hassle them. They should carry a sign that says 'Arrest My Ass.' What's it like where you live?"

"Not so good," I say. "My father left when I was little."

"Man, everybody's father left," Freddie says.

I want to tell him more, about how my mother stopped caring. I want to tell him about Louis, how he moved out and didn't take me with him. And then left me a second time when I got busted. But I say nothing, because my hand starts tapping on the concrete blocks next to the heater panel. Nervous tapping, because of what I might actually say out loud. My arms and legs feel restless and jumpy, too, like I want to get up and walk, but I can't because I'm locked up.

"My home's fucked up, too," says Freddie. "But I'm doing somethin' about it. I got plans."

"Yeah?"

"I passed my GED and applied to community college. Someday I'm gonna get a job working with computers, and I'm gonna buy my own clothes. Nice clothes, too. Then those gay boys will look at me and say, 'Who he?'"

Freddie talks on about his dreams while I try to imagine my own. I try to picture a job and an apartment, but the only thing that sticks is the image of me riding around with Louis in his Bronco. The bass in the subwoofer is thumping out his song, and we're driving to Dimitri's to hang out. I'm going to eat a giant cheeseburger with fries and a chocolate milk shake. I'll ask him if he knows that girl who blew me a kiss and if he can help me find her.

Louis will reach across the empty space between us and put his hand on my shoulder, a single squeeze as if to say, "I'm glad we're driving around together, little bro. No more bad things; we're gonna stick together and look out for each other."

But we're not together and we're not looking out for each other; I am alone in room number fifteen, locked up in the Thomas C. Morton Jr. Residential Center, and I don't know if I'm strong enough to make it out of here.

25

Trouble comes to me in the form of Antwon, the tall, lanky gangbanger with heavy-lidded eyes and the slightest twitch of a smile. He walks across the unit in long, loose strides, moving slowly but effortlessly, like he's going nowhere in particular and has all the time in the world to get there, which I suppose he does.

He sits down next to me, both of us pretending to watch a corny suspense movie on TV.

"What up, James?" he says.

"Nothing," I say. The other boys are curious, watching to see what's going to happen.

Antwon's sleepy eyes show nothing. "I wanna talk some business. Are you cool? You know what I'm saying?"

I want to say, "No, definitely not. What the hell are you saying? Do I look cool to you?" But I don't want to make enemies, and yet I'm not interested in being his friend, either, not even a fake friend. I'm grateful when Tony comes over and takes a nearby chair.

"What's up, Antwon?" he says.

"Having a conversation that don't concern you," says Antwon. "What are you, his big Rican brother?"

"No, I just don't want to hear any of your shit today."

"And I don't wanna hear your shit, either, *comprende?*"

"Yeah, that's good, because I'm leaving soon. How about you? When are you leavin', next year? Year after?"

Antwon shakes his head like he's disappointed by Tony's rudeness. But really it's only because the guards are watching. He stands up, smoothing the edges of his short hair with his fingertips. He gives me a nod. "We'll conversate later, James."

He lopes back across the floor to the Ping-Pong table, where a line of other boys stand waiting for their turn.

"What's that fool want?" says Tony.

"I don't know. Something about business."

"He thinks he's a big shot for his gang. He tries to get all the new guys to rep."

"I don't even know what that means."

"Exactly, 'cause it's bullshit. I'll keep him off you for now, but you probably got to fight him after I get released."

"When's that?"

"Real soon. And I'm a little nervous about it, bro," he says.

"Why?"

"Because in here everybody understands that you gotta *do you,* you know? Just focus on yourself. But at home? Shit. At home everybody I know wants something from me. My girl. My sisters. My mother. My boys. Too much fucking responsibility. You know what I mean?"

"Not really. Nobody expects anything from me."

"That sounds nice. You could, like, relax and shit."

"I suppose."

"Listen, about Antwon. You *do* know how to fight, don't you?"

When I fail to answer, Tony busts out laughing. "I'm sorry, man," he says. "I don't mean no disrespect; it's just a little funny is all. Your white ass coming to Morton all innocent and shit. Don't worry, though; you'll be okay. I know you're tough inside."

26

During free time I stand in line waiting for my turn to play Ping-Pong. Double X has dominated all afternoon. No one can get ten points, much less beat him.

But before I get to the table, Mr. Pike calls me into the staff office. "Phone call," he says, pulling on his red beard, looking at a Time-Life military history book from our classroom library. "You got five minutes. Don't talk about drugs, gangs, or any other illegal activities."

"Okay," I say.

He sits in the swiveling office chair looking at his book, which is about World War II. He pushes the phone in my direction and says, "Clock's running."

I pick up the receiver tentatively, like it's something dangerous, which I suppose it is. Maybe it's my mother. Maybe she left Ron and is calling to see if I'm okay. Maybe she's going to apologize, or tell me she loves me, or something.

"Hello," I say.

"It's me. Louis."

Louis. My big brother, who was supposed to look out for

me. Suddenly I want to curse him out for leaving me and tell him he is not my brother anymore, that I'm better off without him. I want to tell him that I would have stood up for him if *he'd* needed help.

But I don't say any of these things, because he would get mad and hang up, and then I wouldn't have a family anymore. I'd be left with a gray husk of a mother who doesn't call or visit. And Ron with his body odor and rotten teeth. And that would be no kind of family at all. So what I've got is Louis, who might not be as loyal and strong as I thought he was, but at least he called.

"Hi," I say.

"Are you okay?" The tone of his voice is strange, far away and shaky, like it's a bad connection.

"Yeah."

"Good." But it's not a bad connection. I think his voice is cracking and he's on the edge of losing control.

Louis clears his throat. "I'm sorry about what happened." He goes on for a while. Apologizing. Explaining. But none of it matters anymore, because something is happening inside me. Something is hardening and softening as I realize that all of his toughness and confidence is just so much bullshit. In the end, he is like everyone else. He gets scared and makes mistakes. He talks big but fakes it most of the time. And if this is true, which I think it is, then how can I *not* forgive him? I have to, because I would want to be forgiven. I would want him to give me a second chance. Maybe we can both have second chances.

And maybe, when I get out of Morton, the two of us can go far away and start over. Someplace where there aren't any drugs to deliver. No detention centers. No screwed-up mothers or disappeared fathers.

"It's okay, Louis," I say. "Really. I'm fine."

He clears his throat again. "You sure?"

"Yeah," I lie.

"Do you need anything? The guy I talked to said I can come visit next week, if you want." His voice sounds a little stronger, more together.

"Yes, I want you to come. Can you bring me a book?"

"Sure, bro. Any book? You want something special?"

"It's called *The Sea Wolf,* by Jack London."

"You got it. Lemme write it down."

His receiver clatters while he looks for a pen and paper. Mr. Pike points at his watch to let me know that my time is up. He taps the receiver button and disconnects the call. Eyes narrowed, he studies me. For what? Does he actually think I'm some kind of threat? I want to tell him I'm not, that I'm not worth the trouble of pushing around or intimidating.

"Tell me something, James. Are you a smart guy?"

"I guess so," I say, hoping that he'll let me go back to my room. I'm worried that Louis will forget the name of the book, and all I want to do is lie on my bed and listen to the clock tick off the minutes until the visit.

"I don't know," I say at last.

He flashes a fake grin and rubs the red bristles in his beard. "Because Ms. Bonetta showed me a paper you wrote in English class yesterday. It was a nice paper, too, nicest I seen in a place where most kids are half retarded and can't read or write for shit. She said your paper was damn near college level! So tell me, James. Are you smart?"

"I guess I'm smart in English class, sir."

"That's right, you're smart in English class. See, that's a smart answer—you agreed so you and me won't have no conflict. So tell me, why is a smart kid like you getting friendly with someone . . . different like Freddie?"

"I don't know."

"You like *different* people? Is that it?"

"I don't know."

"Well, consider this a warning, James. A friendly warning."

"I don't understand."

"Then let me explain it. Some of them boys out there, like Antwon and Coty and Xavier, ain't as worldly and understanding as I am. They ain't tolerant of *alternative lifestyles* and shit like that. And they been talking about you and Freddie. Wondering. Know what I mean?"

A knot starts to form in my stomach. I see what Pike's doing, but it's too late. Tony tried to warn me, too. "Take care of yourself," he said. "Freddie is on his own."

I nod slowly, careful not to show any emotion.

"Good, because I want to help you do good here and get home. You want my help, don't you?"

I nod again, a little too quickly this time. "Yes. I want your help."

"All right, then."

27

It's the beginning of my second week, and I've learned the schedule and most of the rules. Bobby has returned from Charlie Unit with a blue fiberglass cast. He's picked most of it away, and the dirty cotton lining is hanging off the ends in tatters. He says Charlie Unit sucks even worse than Bravo.

"The guards are bigger douche bags than Horvath and Pike," he says. "Well, almost. And they got this kid that pisses on his radiator every night because he hates being locked in. The whole place smells like piss, but they can't get him to stop."

Today for group Mr. Eboue and Mr. Samson hand out copies of a paperback book with a picture on the cover. It shows a pair of strong black hands wringing out some kind of a rag. There's no face or body, but I think the owner of those hands is angry.

"We're starting a new group," Samson says, tossing the last copies to Freddie and me. The title is *Always Outnumbered, Always Outgunned*, by Walter Mosley. I flip to the end to get a page count: two hundred eight. If I don't read it all at once, I can make it last until Louis's visit on Wednesday.

Right away Wilfred's and Bobby's hands shoot into the air.

"Yes, Wilfred," says Samson.

"Like, whose books are these? They belong to the school or the unit?"

"They're yours," Samson says.

"But what if I don't like it?"

"Then I'll give you your money back," Samson says, winking at me.

Wilfred looks confused. He touches his mustache, says, "But, mister, I didn't pay no money."

"Shut up, fool," says Double X. "He's giving them to us."

"You shut the fuck up," says Wilfred, looking ready to fight. But Mr. Eboue comes over and settles him down with a few whispered words.

It takes a minute for the room to quiet, and then Samson opens the cover. "This is my favorite book," he says. "I'm going to share it with all of you. It's about Socrates Fortlow, an ex-con who murdered two people and spent twenty-seven years in prison. Now he's out on the streets of L.A., trying to see if it's possible for him to become a good man."

"This a true story?" Antwon says.

Samson ignores the question and continues. "He caught this boy, Darryl, killing an old rooster Socrates kept outside his house, and now he's going to make that boy clean, and cook, and eat it."

"Why?" says Coty.

"To teach him responsibility. Because it wasn't his rooster to kill."

Nobody says anything. Samson clears his throat and starts to read an excerpt from the book in a deep, rough voice that no longer sounds like his own:

"*'You should be afraid, Darryl,' Socrates said, reading the boy's eyes. 'I kilt men with these hands. Choked an' broke 'em. I could crush yo' head wit' one hand.' Socrates held out his left palm.*

"*'I ain't afraid'a you,' Darryl said.*

"*'Yes you are. I know you are 'cause you ain't no fool. You seen some bad things out there but I'm the worst. I'm the worst you ever seen.'*"

Samson keeps reading, until we are lost. Spellbound. For the moment, he has become Socrates Fortlow, a giant ex-convict sitting on an overturned trash can in his too-small apartment in Watts. I can picture him, the faded threadbare T-shirt stretched over his big shoulders, beads of sweat standing out on his bald head. And I very well could be Darryl, the skinny boy waiting to eat his plate of dirty rice, green beans, and tough rooster. I keep one eye on the food, and the other on the doorway, wondering if I'll make it out unharmed, or if the big man will crush my skull with his big hands, the ones the other cons used to call rock breakers.

The boy tells of a crime he committed with some friends, a murder. He becomes scared that Socrates will turn him in. Samson reads on: but Socrates says, "*I ain't your warden, li'l brother. I ain't gonna show you to no jail. I'm just*

112

talkin' to ya—one black man to another one. If you don't hear me there ain't nuthin' I could do.'"

I'm pretty sure I could sit here for the rest of the day listening to Samson read. And although he stops at the end of the first chapter, the words of Socrates Fortlow (about the old rooster's crow that was hardly a whisper) stay with me for a long time:

But at least that motherfucker tried.

28

After dinner I wait in line at the Ping-Pong table to get a shot at Double X, who still hasn't lost. I am in luck, because today he's off his game, distracted by the other guys' talk about Moses Rivera, a gangbanger from Brooklyn who is supposedly going to be a famous boxer.

Wilfred, who is ahead of me in line, says, "That dude's bad, like Mike Tyson bad."

"I heard of him," says Bobby. "He's a killing machine when he gets going, like one of them berserkers."

"What's a berserker?" Wilfred says, but everyone ignores him because his questions can go on forever, until no one remembers what we were talking about in the first place.

It's my serve against Double X, and I'm playing really well, but nobody seems to notice; they are too excited about this Rivera guy.

Double X pauses before his serve. "Well, homeboy was in a fight, right? Punched this dude so hard in the face that the dude almost died!" He hits a soft arcing shot, and I smash it back to take the lead for the first time in the game.

Coty fetches the ball for us and says, "I heard he's locked up at Penfield Secure."

"True," says Double X. "True. But he assaulted a guard, so guess what? Homeboy getting transferred here!" He is excited because this will bump him up in standing within his gang if he can buddy up with Moses, or so Freddie says.

I rip a serve across his backhand. He connects but sprays it wide off the table, ending the game. This means that I am the new Bravo Unit champion, at least until someone beats me. It's the first time I've been good at something, but nobody seems to care right now. Double X hands his paddle to Wilfred, grinning even though he's just been dethroned.

They keep talking about Moses like he's a superhero. Moses is going to kick the guards' asses and free us. Moses is going to bitch slap Horvath and Pike and force them to serve us pizzas in the staff break room. Moses is going to bring down Division of Youth Services with his righteous fists.

I listen to the stories, but I don't care about Moses Rivera. I've got too many things going on in my own head to think about a gangland savior coming to Morton to fight it out with Horvath and the other guards. I'm thinking about my mother and if she's ever going to call or visit. Probably not. Maybe she's sick or something. I try to stop worrying, but I can't. Not in here, at least. In my room at bedtime I listen to the clock hammering away. I count out five hundred ticks. When I get tired of that, I put my ear to the crack in the door to listen to the guards.

Horvath says, "You know that Rivera kid, the boxer?"

"Yeah. So?" says Pike.

"I heard he's coming here. Next week."

"Waste of taxpayer money, if you ask me. He's a real specimen, though. Benches, like, three-fifty."

"He's just a punk," says Horvath. "First time he talks shit, he'll hit the floor just like everyone else."

"Tune him up good."

"That's right."

Pike's laugh, high-pitched and wheezy, makes my skin crawl, and later I dream of hitting the floor.

29

All day I look forward to Louis's visit, but he never shows. Doesn't call, either. Part of me knew he'd blow it off, but I still hoped. I mean, to get off the unit for a couple of hours and talk to my brother . . . it would have been nice. *Fuck it,* I think. *No, fuck him. Fuck Louis and all of his bullshit.*

The rest of the day drags until we go to the gym to play basketball. Freddie and I are the last ones picked because we're terrible at sports. Every time I get the ball, Mr. Pike blows the whistle for double dribbling or traveling. Freddie knows how to dribble, but he misses the entire backboard whenever he shoots. The only player who is worse is Oskar, the Dr. Seuss kid. Oskar spends a lot of time with the psychologist, Dr. Souza. Other times he sleeps or just stares at his hands.

The one occasion I catch a pass, Antwon sticks out his foot, and I go sprawling across the floor. The ball bounces loose and rolls over to Oskar, who is standing at the edge of the game watching us with his big vacant eyes. He looks at the ball blankly and then bends down to pick it up.

The rest of us watch to see what he will do; even Horvath and Pike seem curious. Oskar holds the ball, staring back at us. He bounces it with both of his hands, like a little kid, smiling. Slowly he makes his way toward his own team's basket, and we all back away to clear a lane. When he's close enough, Oskar holds the ball between his legs and launches it up into the air. Incredibly, it bounces off the backboard and drops neatly into the hoop without touching the rim. He turns to look at us, eyes still empty.

Tony claps once, then again. He shoots us all a look that says we'd better clap, too; we do. Oskar tries to smile, but it comes out forced and crooked. He tries to laugh, but it comes out in big choking sobs. He shuffles off the court and starts banging his head on the concrete block wall. He does it hard enough to split open his forehead, smearing blood on the white industrial paint. By the time the guards realize what is happening, Oskar has slid down onto his knees and is rocking back and forth, crying, a thick stream of blood running down his face. It drips off his chin and pools on the green rubber floor. Horvath and Pike move in on him slowly, like confused wrestlers, trying to figure out what to do with an opponent who has just flopped to the mat and pinned himself. They're not sure if they should restrain him or try to help him. But how do you help someone like Oskar? Now he is sitting, completely still, looking intently at his hands.

"Line up!" Mr. E hustles us out of the gym, straight to the cafeteria without showering or changing. When we come back to the unit, Oskar's room is empty. A box of his belongings has been placed outside his door; I peek inside and see a pile of his books. *Horton Hears a Who!* sits on top.

"Where'd he go?" I ask.

"Mental hospital," says Tony.

"For, like, the tenth fucking time," says Bobby. "Kid's bat shit crazy."

"Shut up, Bobby," Tony says.

"You ain't the boss of me!"

"No, but shut up anyway."

And, for once, Bobby does.

30

Tonight Mr. E and Samson throw a pizza party for the whole unit to celebrate Tony's release. The two guards pay for a movie and food with their own money. Levon, a football player from Queens, asks if they're going to do the same for him.

"Sure," Samson says. "When you get your Honors Stage."

Levon groans. "Ain't none of us ever getting Honors Stage. Tony just a freak."

"Speak for yo'self," says Wilfred. "I got four good days behind me."

Samson laughs and tells Wilfred that he is off to a good start but he'll need eighty-six more good days.

The movie is *Transformers II,* which everyone seems to like. Even Antwon, who hates everything. Or at least that's what he'd like us to believe.

"I'll take that yellow Camaro," he says. "That's tight."

Predictably, Double X and Coty agree.

We all get two slices of pizza, a cup of soda, and a piece of chocolate cake that Tony's mother sent in for the occasion. He says that his entire family drove up from New York City and is staying at a fancy Holiday Inn, just so they can pick him up early in the morning.

"They don't want me to ride in no transport van, so they borrowed my uncle's Lincoln. They gonna take me home in style!"

Antwon says that Lincolns are crap, but Tony doesn't take the bait.

"Y'all can say whatever you want," says Tony. "Because tomorrow I'm free. No more Morton for me. No more nasty-ass chili dogs and sandwiches made from government cheese and the bad parts of animals that don't even exist. You know, like them bologna animals and meat loaf animals."

Samson laughs. "What's the first thing you're going to do when you get home?"

"I'm gonna eat my mom's cooking," he says. "Then I'm gonna see my girl, and then my homeboys. Don't worry, Samson. I ain't gonna party or nothing. But I'm not living like a monk, neither!"

Before lights-out Mr. E says, "Right now I have something to say to Tony, but you all might want to hear it, too. If not, that's fine; you can go get ready for bed."

No one moves.

"One of the things I like about people is that everybody has their own story. Doesn't matter if it's a lawyer, or a cop, or somebody's mother cleaning office buildings or

121

working as a home health aide. And all of *you* have stories, too, even if you don't realize it. But right now I want to tell you mine."

"I come to the United States when I was thirteen. From Grenada, a small island. My family was broke so we lived in the projects and got everything from the Goodwill: shoes, clothes, furniture. Even the knickknacks and the pictures on the wall."

There is a chorus of uh-huhs from kids who know this part from their own experiences.

"Me and my cousin, Raymond, got our asses kicked every single day because we had secondhand clothes and Caribbean accents that the other kids said were stuck-up. Then we joined a gang and no one messed with us. We had friends and respect."

Coty, Double X, Levon, and Antwon all say, "Yeah, I hear that," and "True, true."

Mr. Eboue continues, "Until I got busted and locked up. At a place just like this, but it's closed now because a kid was killed there."

"Who kilt him?" says Wilfred. Mr. E ignores him and continues.

"I followed the rules in lockup, but I didn't learn anything. So when I got out, I thought I had outsmarted the system. But what I didn't know is that the system doesn't care if you change. The system is like a machine; all it cares about is its gears and levers and shit. Input and output. If you do six months and earn your stage, you go home. Lots of kids are getting arrested and the system needs your bed? That means you go home whether you're ready or not."

"So everything was cool until I got off the bus in Brooklyn and learned that my cousin, Raymond, had been shot dead in some gang shit. Nobody told me!"

"Why not?" Wilfred says.

"Because they thought I'd flip out and do something self-destructive, which is probably true."

Levon says that his cousin got shot last year. Danny, a white kid from Schenectady, says his little brother was stabbed but didn't die. He's in a wheelchair now. Other kids say who in their family was killed. Mr. E waits patiently until they're done.

"I didn't believe that Raymond was dead. 'Show me!' I said to my mother, who is only, like, five feet tall and was working two jobs to pay for rent and food for me and my brothers and sisters. By that time, my father had split and started a whole new family someplace else, but that's a whole nother kind of story. My mother just cried and took me to my old bedroom that I used to share with my cousin."

"What'd you see?" says Wilfred again.

"Pictures from his funeral. She had them up on the walls like a shrine. 'It was a nice funeral,' she said. 'You would have been proud.'"

Mr. E takes a moment to breathe. He touches the corner of his eye with a hand. "Man, I went off the train tracks for a long time. And let's just say that I did some things, and that I was lucky I didn't get locked up again. Or killed."

"Did you find the dudes that done it?" Coty says.

Mr. E waves off the question with a hand and continues.

"But when it was all done, when I was done *reacting* . . . to this thing that I couldn't accept, I realized that the only difference between me and my cousin was that I got locked up. I was off the streets when the guns came out. Otherwise, I'd be dead, too."

Wilfred raises his hand. "No offense, Mr. E, but what's this story mean? That it's good to be locked up so you don't get shot?"

"It means that you're all marked and you have to try to live the rest of your life so you're not around violence."

Wilfred nods, but he still looks confused.

Before bed Tony says his goodbyes; he'll be leaving early in the morning while we're all still asleep. Handshakes or hugs aren't allowed, so he gathers up his personal items, which are a bundle of papers and a few family pictures.

"Y'all take care of yourselves," he says. To Mr. E and Samson he says, "I'm gonna make you guys proud of me."

"Do that by having a good life and not coming back," says Samson.

"James," Tony says before I go into my room. "You remember what I told you, bro?"

I give him the thumbs-up sign to show that I remember: take care of myself, fight Antwon, and let Freddie deal with his own problems.

"Thanks for the free advice," I say.

"No problem. Have a nice life, man."

"You too."

31

Every Saturday we're allowed to sleep in until nine o'clock, but I am awake at six, cursing my brother. Yesterday, he finally got around to calling to apologize for missing our visit. "Something came up, bro," he said. "Next week. I promise." Like I'm going to believe that.

So I stare out the window at the razor wire fence and the parking lot. I watch the seven-to-three staff park their Chevy Tahoes and Silverados, Ford F-150 pickups, and big Harley-Davidson motorcycles. They carry giant cups of coffee and bags of hash browns and Egg McMuffin sandwiches from McDonald's.

The big wall-mounted clock hammers out time while, beyond my door, Horvath and Pike talk through the final hour of the eleven-to-seven shift they picked up for overtime. They are talking just to talk, to keep themselves awake. And if I didn't know any better from what happened the other day with Bobby, I would think of them as just a couple of regular guys staying up late bullshitting, instead of hateful assholes in charge of the lives of a bunch of kids.

"You ever play baseball when you were a kid?" Horvath says.

"Yep. Wasn't no good, though."

"I played catcher."

"You look like a catcher. Bet you wore them husky-sized kid jeans, right?"

Horvath ignores the joke. "My old man was the coach. He said the catcher controls the game."

They are silent for a moment before Horvath picks up the thread of his story. I'm surprised that he even *has* a story; none of the adults I have known—not my mother, or even Mr. Pfeffer—have talked about their pasts. In a way, I don't want to know more about Mr. Horvath, because I don't want to understand why he is a bastard. As far as I'm concerned, he's the biggest piece of shit I've ever met next to Ron. But at the same time, hearing him talk about his childhood is oddly compelling, like wanting to see a car wreck. So I keep my ear pressed to the door.

"My last year in Babe Ruth, we made it to the state championships. My old man told us the other team was better but that talent didn't matter; what mattered was heart. He said if we wanted it bad enough, if we had the heart, we'd win."

"What happened?"

"We got behind early and spent the whole game trying to catch up. But I tied it up with a three-run homer in the eighth."

"You won?"

"Lost in the bottom of the ninth. Last time I ever played ball."

126

"Man, that sucks. But at least you made it that far. That's something."

"My old man didn't think so. To him you were a winner or a loser; there wasn't no in-between. He drove the whole way home without saying a word."

"He didn't say nothin'?"

"Nope. Not one word."

"No offense, but he sounds like a big asshole. That ain't no way to treat your kid. And you got a home run, too! Fucking-A, Horvath."

I look out the small rectangular window set in my door. I can see Pike holding up his hand for a high five, but his partner leaves him hanging.

"Shut your mouth, Pike," he says. "He was my father, and you're missing the point."

"All right, what's the point?"

"That I showed him respect. And none of these entitled delinquent pussies knows how to do that. Not the street thugs, the nutcases, or the ones who are just stupid. Freddie Peach is the worst, because he's gonna go on and 'Yes, sir' everyone and get his privileges without learning a fucking thing. In and out in ninety days. You wait and see."

"I hear that. It's like he thinks he's better than everyone else. Makes me sick to look at these queers on TV running around flaunting their perversions, like it's a constitutional right or something."

But Horvath isn't listening. He's leaning back in his chair, hands laced behind his thick neck, staring at some distant point on the concrete block wall in front of him.

Pike tries again. "It ain't like the old days, before all this therapeutic bullshit."

Horvath drops the legs of his chair with a thud and rolls his heavy shoulders forward. He looks focused, no longer lost in memories of his father and the state Babe Ruth championship. "You know what I think, Pike?" he says.

"Negative, Horvath. Tell me."

"Everybody gets what's coming to them. That's my philosophy, and Freddie's gonna get his. He'll run his mouth one too many times."

Pike smiles, happy to finish the shift on a positive note. "And when he does . . ."

But I don't get to hear the rest, because the door to the unit opens; Crupier and a guard from a different unit come in, ready to start their shift.

32

Today we all get two stamps and envelopes for letter writing, which we're allowed to do during school. I write one really short letter to my mother, telling her I'm okay and listing the phone number for Morton, along with the times she can call (even though I know she won't).

The other letter is for Mr. Pfeffer. It goes like this:

Dear Mr. Pfeffer,

I'm sorry I haven't come to your class lately, but I did something bad and got locked up in this place called the Thomas C. Morton Jr. Residential Center, which is what most people would call juvie. Maybe you already know this, but it's possible no one told you, in which case I'd like for you to hear it from me. I didn't hurt anyone or steal, but what I did was wrong and I deserve to be here. Morton is not a very good place to be, except for Mr.

Samson, who is a bodybuilder and quotes books,
too. I think you'd like him.

Anyway, I wanted to thank you for all the early-
morning talks, cold root beers, and great books.
You're the best teacher. Ever. If you have time to
write me back, it would mean a lot—but I know
you're probably busy.

Sincerely,
James
Your Student

Later, at three o'clock, we have group. Mr. E says to the
circle of fidgeting boys, "Let's say you're getting onto a bus
or a subway, and it's really crowded."

Wilfred, who seems to do everything slowly—walking,
talking, thinking—raises one of his big hands halfway into
the air. Yesterday I heard Mr. Eboue tell him he had the
fingers of a jazz piano player, and Wilfred said, "Is that
good?"

"You have a question already, Wilfred?"

"Yes, mister, I do." Despite being at Morton for almost
a year (according to Freddie), he still can't remember any
of the staff's names.

"Okay, shoot."

"What I want to know, mister, is if it's a subway or a
bus."

"Whichever, Wilfred. Doesn't matter."

"But it matters to *me*, mister, because I'm trying to picture it in my head. If it's a bus, then I'll be standing at the

bus stop, freezing. But if it's the subway, then I be inside the mall entrance, watching to see when the train pulls up."

Mr. E sighs and says, "Let's go with the subway, Wilfred, so you can stay warm."

Wilfred smiles and sits back in his chair, satisfied.

"So, you're about to get on the train, and some dude jumps out and steps right on your new Jordans, the ones you bought with your own hard-earned money."

Levon, Double X, and Antwon groan to show how bad it would be to get your new Jordans stepped on.

Mr. E says, "It's the first time you ever wore those shoes, and the brother doesn't say 'Sorry,' or 'Excuse me,' or nothing. He looks you in the eye and walks past, like you're a punk. Worse than a punk because you don't even get so much as a glare. It's like he doesn't even recognize you exist."

Several of the guys say they'd give him an ass whooping.

"It's a matter of respect for yourself," says Antwon. "Because if you act like it's okay, then nobody going to respect you, and you ain't even going to respect yourself, which is worse, 'cause it gives you, like, this smell in the streets where other people can tell that you're weak."

Everybody else agrees, but I'm not sure. I haven't had an expensive pair of sneakers. But if I did, I wouldn't fight someone just because they stepped on them. It seems stupid, but the other guys see it differently.

"Show of hands," Mr. E says. "How many of you would give the homeboy a beat-down?"

All hands shoot up in the air except for mine.

Mr. E pretends to be surprised. "Freddie, you too?"

"Just because I'm *G-A-Y* don't mean I'm a pussy. I *know* how to fight, Mr. E."

Everybody laughs.

"That's funny, Freddie, and I hear what you're saying, but please don't talk like that."

"It's true, and I ain't ashamed no more," he says.

"I'm glad, Freddie, but even so . . ."

"Okay. Sorry, Mr. E."

"Wilfred?" says Mr. E to get us back on track.

"I throw down, mister. Nobody step on my Jordans." He slaps the back of one extra large hand against the palm of the other for emphasis.

Levon eggs him on. "You git him, Wilfred!"

Wilfred looks angry and fired up, like he's really on the streets in his newly scuffed Jordans. He stands and starts a slow, loose shadowboxing sequence with his giant half-closed fists. "You *know* I will, Levon! That's just me doing me, you know what I mean?"

Hooting and cheering ring out, and it takes a while for Mr. E and Samson to settle everyone down. In a moment Wilfred remembers where he is; he looks around, embarrassed, then takes his seat.

"Okay. Now imagine that you've just been released. You're on aftercare, and probation. And your family needs you at home to help out. So if you get in a fight with this dude, it's back to lockup. And the folks who are counting on you will be sad and disappointed."

Everyone groans with the difficulty of this twist.

"Well, how about it?"

"That ain't fair," Antwon says.

"You set it up!" says Levon.

"Yo, that's messed up!" Double X says.

Before we're dismissed for free time, Mr. E says, "I want you all to think about it for a few days, and then I want to hear your answers."

33

After group, Samson asks Freddie and me to stay back. "Either of you know what I want to talk to you about?"

We look at each other, shaking our heads.

"We had a treatment team meeting yesterday and scored your behavior checklists. Congratulations. You both got your A-Stage."

A-Stage, or "Adjustment Stage," is what you can get after three weeks of good days. To go home, you have to earn Transition Stage. You also need a positive home assessment, which means there's enough room for you in the apartment, food in the fridge, etc. Honors is the highest stage, but Tony was the only resident in the last two years to earn it.

Samson hands us a folder that's filled with take-out menus for pizza, Chinese food, and subs. "This Friday is Stage Night," he says. "If you guys have enough money from chores and want to order out, write it down and I'll take care of it. And decide what you want to do after. We can watch a movie, go to the gym, whatever. Until someone else gets it together and earns their stage, it's just the three of us."

On our way back to the unit, Samson says, "You guys are doing a good job. Keep it up and you'll be going home soon."

Freddie and I pore over the menus during free time. We weigh the merits of pizza and wings versus chicken Parmesan subs versus egg rolls and shrimp lo mein. Freddie is obsessed with food and talks forever about the best restaurants in Harlem.

"There's this one place," he says, "where they got these things called bento boxes that have little compartments filled with different kinds of Chinese foods, like tempura vegetables, and sushi rolls, and teriyaki chicken and shit. You have to eat it all with chopsticks, which is harder than it looks, but I'm good at it."

He gets this far-off dreamy look on his face, but he says, "I like Asian food, but it don't fill you up like plain old pizza and wings."

"Okay," I say. "We'll have that."

"Cool. You like Hawaiian pizza? I love that shit. We can get a large Hawaiian pizza; that's four big slices each, and then three or four dozen wings. How many wings you eat?"

"Hawaiian pizza's disgusting," I say. "How about sausage and pepperoni?"

"With black olives?"

We shake on the deal, forgetting for a moment that in Morton residents can't shake hands, bump fists, hug, horseplay, or have any other kind of physical contact with each other. It says so on the first page of the resident handbook and is followed by a list of consequences including a formal write-up and temporary loss of privileges. Maybe we forget because the guards have been preoccupied with the baseball game that is on TV, or maybe it's because we're having fun for a minute, feeling like normal kids instead of criminals. But right away Horvath's voice booms across the unit floor.

"Why are you two touching each other?" he says.

The room gets cold, and I can feel the eyes of the other boys on Freddie and me. Coty and Double X are pointing, whispering. Antwon mouths the word *homo*.

"We wasn't," says Freddie. "We was just shaking hands 'cause—"

"Save it," Horvath says. "Nobody wants to hear the details, so just keep your perversions to yourself."

Now the whole unit is laughing. Horvath is laughing, too. "You two can be special friends at home if you want, but not on my unit. Got it?"

I am turning deep red from embarrassment, but I can't help it. Freddie puts his hands palms-down on the table and breathes slowly, trying to keep calm. I know that I have nothing to be ashamed of, that we're not *special friends*, but the shame burns through me nonetheless. It's crazy, but I feel totally guilty, like I've been caught doing something bad.

"I got it," I say.

"Good," says Horvath. "Now how about you, Peachy?"

He hesitates just enough to let Horvath know that he's

got some fight in him, that he's not going to play along so easily because Horvath has a uniform and keys. Finally he says, "I got it."

And we are spared the disgrace of losing our stages only minutes after getting them. Horvath appears satisfied, or maybe just more interested in the game. He grunts and returns to the TV.

34

At dinner on Friday (spaghetti and meatballs with buttered white bread) Antwon lines up behind me at the counter. "Yo," he says. "Now that your spic big brother ain't here, we gonna have that talk."

"Okay," I say. "No problem." But I have no idea what to do. I can put him off for another day or two, but sooner or later I'll have to deal with it. Gratefully, Samson pulls Freddie and me from the line and takes us for Stage Night.

"Did you two fools forget?" he says.

"No way," says Freddie. "I didn't eat none of that nasty spaghetti, 'cause I know we're havin' the good stuff."

"That's right," says Samson. "You thought about what you want to do for an activity?"

"Let James pick," Freddie says. "All I care about is eatin'."

Samson raises an eyebrow, waiting.

"Can you show me how to lift weights?"

"Absolutely," he says. "Come on."

We spend the next hour in the weight room. Freddie sits on the exercise bike and watches television while Samson starts me out on the bench press. He shows me how to grip the bar and plant my feet flat on the ground. He tells me how to breathe the right way, exhaling when I push the weight up.

"Okay," he says. "See if you can do fifteen using just the bar. It weighs forty-five pounds."

It's easy at first, but toward the end my arms get weak and shaky. After a short rest he puts twenty pounds on each side. "Do as many as you can," he says. I make it to five before my chest and arms are burning with fatigue. He has me finish up with fifteen more using just the bar.

"How do you feel?" he says.

"Weak."

"Yeah, but aside from that, how do you feel?"

"Pretty good. Like I'm doing something good for myself." I can't help smiling, because it's true.

Samson puts his hand on my shoulder and says, "That's right. You did do something good for yourself."

Then he shows me how to do squats for my legs, dips for my triceps, and two different kinds of curls for biceps. "I'll work with you every Friday," he says, "so long as you keep your stage. Any questions?"

"You think I can get stronger?"

"Absolutely," he says. "You'll see."

We finish the night eating take-out pizza and Buffalo wings. Freddie devours an entire piece of pizza in two bites. The wings he eats whole, pulling clean bones from his mouth. Soon there's a small pile of them.

"Damn," Samson says. "You're a professional, Freddie!"

But Freddie doesn't even slow down long enough to smile, or to wipe the hot sauce smeared on his face. One of the lenses of his glasses sports a fingerprint of grease. I think back to the van ride from court, how his nice white shirt was covered with food stains. As I watch him polish off the rest of the wings and all of the celery and blue cheese, I realize that he's doing something he truly loves. He smiles placidly as he sits back in his chair and sighs.

"My fat ass is finally happy," he says. "Thank you, Samson."

"Yes," I say. "Thank you."

But he shrugs it off as though giving Freddie his best meal in months is no big deal. As though teaching me how to get strong isn't the thing I've wanted from my big brother, Louis, for so long.

Later, in bed, my arms and chest and legs are warm with the mild burn of my workout. It feels good, and I drift off to sleep easily, almost peacefully, for the moment forgetting all about Antwon and his boys.

35

After school we grab our Walter Mosley books and sit in a circle. Mr. Eboue and Samson sit with us.

"You guys are reading, right?" says Wilfred.

"I'll read," says Samson. "But today I want one of you to do Darryl's part. You up for it, Wilfred? It's just a few lines."

"No disrespect, Mr. Samson, but I don't read like that, out loud. I just want to hear about Socrates."

Antwon, Double X, and Bobby mutter that they won't read, either.

"Somebody's got to step up," says Mr. Eboue. "Who's feeling brave today?"

I raise my hand.

"Good man," says Mr. Eboue. We start reading this chapter called "Lessons," where Darryl fights a gang-banger named Philip who's been after him at school. Darryl puts up a good fight, but in the end, Philip has him pinned to the ground with a .45 automatic. Around me the boys seem to love the action, especially when Socrates sneaks up on Philip's friends and slaps them so hard on the backs of their heads that they fall down and drop their weapons. Double X laughs out loud when Philip calls Darryl "pussy boy."

"He *is* a pussy boy," says Antwon, looking right at me. Samson holds up a finger and moves it slowly back and forth. Antwon sucks his teeth, but looks down at his book.

Samson reads the part where after the fight, Socrates says, *"'You stood up for yourself, Darryl . . . that's all a black man could do. You always outnumbered, you always outgunned.'"*

And even though Samson's reading from a book, it feels like he's really speaking to me. I'm not a black man, and I haven't fought anyone, but I still feel proud, because Samson is someone I respect. Maybe one day I'll hear those words for real.

Most of the guys think Socrates is right, and that you have to shoot first and hit harder.

"The chapter's called 'Lessons,' right?" says Levon. "So that means you got to teach a punk like Philip the lesson before he teaches it to you."

Mr. E and Samson try to make it a serious conversation, but everyone keeps blurting out stupid shit.

"My boys wouldn't let no old man sneak up on them," says Antwon.

"I'd take Philip's gun and pop him with it," says Bobby.

"Yeah, you know it, little man," says Wilfred.

"Don't call me that, mouth breather," says Bobby.

When Samson gets control, he says, "Don't you ever feel like the rules are stacked against you? Like you can't win, no matter how hard you try?"

It's quiet for a moment, and then we're all nodding our heads, saying, "Yeah, yeah, it does feel like that." Wilfred swears that he's been doing his best at Morton for eleven months, and he isn't even close to earning his stage. Bobby says he's never going to pass the TABE test and qualify for GED prep.

Near the end of group Samson reads a scene where Socrates is cooking chicken and rice gumbo for Darryl over a camp stove: *"'He wished that some man had had that kind of love for him before he'd gone wrong . . . He was a troubled child with no father; one of those lost souls who did wrong but didn't know it—or hardly did.'"*

"What's this mean?" says Mr. Eboue.

I raise my hand. "That Socrates might have turned out different if someone had loved him and taught him to be a man." I half expect the other guys to laugh, for Antwon to call me a pussy boy. But they don't. Nobody says anything for a long time.

Finally, Freddie breaks the silence. "That's deep."

"Yeah," says Levon, "mad deep."

36

Another Wednesday, which is visitation day, and I can't stop thinking about Louis. After all that's happened, he can't make the effort to come see me or even write a damn letter. How much would it take him to write a letter? Less than is needed to blow me off, I'm sure.

But then Pike bangs on my door. "James," he says, "you got a visitor. Come on."

Before I can even think about it, he leads me to a small windowless room. Sports posters line the walls, along with corny motivational slogans like THERE IS NO I IN TEAM and A QUITTER NEVER WINS AND A WINNER NEVER QUITS.

Louis sits in a fabric waiting-room chair. He's wearing a plain black T-shirt that stretches tight over his shoulders and biceps. Physically he looks the same, but something is different about the way he carries himself. It's not like his posture is slumped or anything; it's more subtle than that, but I can't put my finger on it.

Pike sizes Louis up and stiffens a little the way dogs do when they're trying to decide who is alpha.

"You James's brother?" says Pike.

"Louis." He offers his hand, but Pike doesn't take it. Instead the guard stands with his arms crossed, scowling at Louis, who is obviously bigger and stronger. But he doesn't have the uniform. Or the radio. Or the cuffs. And in here that means something.

"Maybe you can talk some sense into your little brother before he goes down a bad road."

"I thought he was doing okay."

"Who told you that?"

"African guy. Mr. E-something. On the phone. He said James earned his stage and would be eligible for early release."

"Eboue." Pike says it like he's got a bad taste in his mouth. "Did he tell you that kids lose their stages all the time? You should ask James about his new friend. Let's just say his *friend* is a bad influence."

Louis digests this. "Can we have our visit now?" he says. And a tiny bit of pride swells in me to see how Louis handles someone like Pike. He might not keep his promises, or give two shits about me, but still . . . he doesn't let the assholes of the world mess with him.

Pike hooks his thumbs into his belt loops. "Go ahead. I'll be outside."

When we're alone, Louis says, "What's his problem?"

"Everything."

"God, what an asshole," he says. "I don't know how you can stand it here."

"It's not like I have a choice, you know."

The comment hangs in the air, until Louis slides a

paperback across the table. "I brought your book," he says.

I look at the cover of the ship crashing through a dark sea. I pick it up and hold it; it feels good in my hands, like a Bible might to a religious person. I've got the Walter Mosley book in my room, and now I've got this one. It's only two books, I know, but it feels like I'm building my own library of great books that are going to help me. I'm going to spend every spare moment reading them, until I find what Samson and Mr. Pfeffer want me to see. I'd like to stop the visit right now. I could go back to my room, bury my head in the pages of the book, and disappear for a few hours. Louis can go home or to Dirk's Gym or wherever the hell he wants. He can feel good about himself because he drove out here to see me and did his brotherly duty.

But I stay in my seat. "Thanks."

He looks away.

"How's everything at home?" I say.

"Fucked up. The Bronco's gone for good. I still owe money."

I nod, but I don't really care. I know how he feels about that thing, but I'd trade ten Broncos to get out of here. "You seen Mom?"

"You know I don't go over there."

"Does she even care that I'm here?"

"Honestly, I don't know what she cares about." He tugs at the collar of his T-shirt as though it's choking him. "Listen, James. I'm sorry."

It's strange to hear him say that. I've never heard him

apologize. For anything. How can you live nineteen years without ever once being wrong?

"It's okay," I say. But the truth is, I'm not sure if it's okay. I need to think. Things are different now and I'm not going to follow Louis blindly just because I want to be cool. Those days are over.

"No. It's not." He takes a deep breath and closes his eyes. His words come out haltingly and shaky. "It's *not* okay. I'm your brother. I'm not supposed to set you up."

"I knew what I was getting into."

"No, you didn't."

And I begin to wonder, because his eyes are filled with terror, like he's about to tell me something bad, something that will change everything forever. Like the time he told me our father was leaving for good. I had only known him as a man who was sometimes home, sometimes not. But he always brought us presents, cheap balsa gliders, cap guns, and rubber balls that bounced super high. He'd pull up to the house in his white Jeep Comanche, and we'd all run out to the porch to greet him. And then, a few days later, he'd be gone. It's funny, but I remember the presents more than I remember him.

When Louis first told me he wasn't ever coming back, I said, "I don't believe you."

"Doesn't matter," said Louis. "He's still not coming back. Mom says."

"Why?"

"I don't know. Maybe he doesn't love us anymore."

"Who'll take care of us?"

"I will. I'm the man of the house now, and you'd better listen."

Louis was right. He never did come back, no matter how many times I watched the driveway for his pickup. And my mother fell into a routine of work, smoking cigarettes, and bringing home different loser guys, the most recent of which was Ron. And now, locked up in Morton, my brother wants to tell me something else that's big and important. What is it, that he's leaving for good? That I'm on my own? Because if it's the second thing, I already know it. I'll tell him that I figured it out all by myself.

37

"Vern didn't join the marines," says Louis.

I wait to hear the rest, blood thrumming in my temples. Of course he didn't join the damn marines. I knew that. But I accepted the lie, because I didn't want to know the truth. Because I wasn't strong enough. And now he's going to tell me? Part of me wants to tell him to get the fuck out, before he says another word. I can live without his self-serving version of the truth. But the other part of me wants to know. Needs to know.

"He got locked up at Five Points. For possession with intent to sell, and also conspiracy. Three to five years, but he'll do the max because he didn't rat on me."

I am stunned.

Louis is talking fast now, trying to get it all out. "The cops were trying to nail me, but they got Vern instead. They were watching and following all the time. And they thought Vern would roll on me."

"But he didn't?"

"No. He was solid. Like you. Strong."

"I'm not strong," I say, even though I'm trying to be.

He shakes his head to correct me; his eyes are teary. I'm trying to understand what he's saying. Louis let his friend go down for him, and then set me up to take his place. All the time knowing that the cops were watching, waiting. It explains a lot of what the detective guy said, how they really wanted Louis, not me.

"I know how it sounds." He looks away from me, pretending to focus on the motivational poster by a famous athlete that says I'VE MISSED ONE HUNDRED PERCENT OF THE SHOTS I DIDN'T TAKE. What do those words even mean?

I stare at the poster, trying to think straight. Does he know how messed up it is that Vern is in prison and I'm in Morton? He should leave right now and never talk to me again. I should tell him this. I should tell him that he's not my brother anymore. But I don't, because everything's changing and I'm confused. I thought Louis was strong. I thought he cared about me. But a strong person doesn't let his best friend and his brother go to jail. And a strong person doesn't turn his back on his mother. Because even if she makes mistakes, even if she's really messed up and drunk all the time, even if she chooses to be with a guy like Ron, she's still his mother.

How many other things has Louis lied to me about? I think back to that time on Louis's BMX bike, riding on the handlebars with my arms outstretched. "King of the world," he said. Was that real? Did it actually happen, or is it another thing I just want to believe?

"You can tell them the truth," he says. "I don't care anymore. Maybe I deserve to be locked up."

I am on the verge of crying or throwing up. Or maybe I'm going to bang my head against the concrete block wall, like Oskar. It doesn't seem so crazy now. Maybe that's how you get rid of bad thoughts.

"Why didn't you help me?" The question sputters out of me like a sick cough.

He shrugs his shoulders. How useless are those big muscles when they're gifted to a coward? The words form in my head: *Louis, my big brother, is a coward.*

"I was scared," he says.

"What?" There's an edge to my voice that's never been there before. *I'm* questioning *him.*

"I said I was scared." He's sniffling, wiping at his nose.

"Scared of what? You're Louis! What do you have to be afraid of? You're tough and cool. Everybody wants to be like you. *I* wanted to be like you!"

"But you don't anymore," he says. "I understand. You shouldn't."

"What are you afraid of?"

"A lot of things. Like going to prison. I can't do time, James. No way." He sniffs again. "After Dad left, I told myself I wasn't going to count on anyone ever again. I'd look out for myself. Make my own money."

We sit in silence. A river of emotions burns hot and fast through me, and then suddenly I am empty, staring at the faded motivational poster, wondering what happened to all my feelings. Where did they go?

After some time I say, "I'm not going to rat you out, Louis." The words sound absolute, pushed out with conviction and a weird power. My hands and fingers feel strange,

151

like they're not my own, and I wiggle them in front of my face, rubbing and pinching them to get some feeling back. Am I going crazy? No. I'm not going crazy. I am changing. Growing up. Getting stronger. I am in the visitation room with Louis, telling him how it's going to be from now on.

"I won't rat you out," I say. "But I'm not doing it for you. I'm doing it for me."

"What the fuck are you talking about, James?" He's looking at me different, like I'm someone other than his stupid, gullible brother.

"I'm standing up for myself from now on. I'm going to learn how to be brave. It's in the book you brought me."

"I don't know what you're talking about. It's a crap adventure book."

But I'm through explaining myself to him. I don't care if he doesn't understand. I rise and knock on the door to get the attention of Pike, who is outside talking up one of the female guards. He opens the door to the visitation room.

"Go to Central Services," he says to Louis, pointing toward the small room separated by a thick tempered glass window and sliding steel drawer. "They'll get your keys and things."

"I'm not finished talking to my brother." Louis stands up with no small amount of attitude.

Pike stops, the challenge registering on his face in the form of a thin smile.

"You're finished if I say you are, buddy."

Out of nowhere Horvath and Crupier materialize.

They flank Pike, making him appear much larger than his actual size. Three guards as one.

"What's the problem, Byron?" Horvath plants his big black combat boots in a wide stance, hands on hips.

"Nothing I can't handle," says Pike. "Croop, take James back to Bravo. Me and Horvath will stay and go over the rules with big brother."

I see the flash of fire in Louis's eyes. He wants to pummel the small man in front of him and set things right in the world. "I am fighting for you, James," he could say after. "I do care about you." But he knows it's too late for that. He takes a step back and shows his hands in surrender. "You guys are in charge here," he says. "I'm leaving."

"That's right you're leaving." The guards follow him out the door and then crack jokes, calling him "pretty boy" and my "faggot big brother."

38

The rest of the day is a fog, and I have no appetite. I'm locked up while Louis is driving home to his apartment, where he can play *Call of Duty* on his Xbox in front of his big-screen television, or else he'll go to Dirk's Gym and bench-press three big plates on each side, 350 pounds, while all the blond spandex girls with amazing bodies flirt with him and admire his muscles and tattoos.

"Yo," Coty says. "We seen your brother getting checked in before your visit. He's a big dude. He's, like, ripped, and he got that killer look in his face. So what happened to you?"

"Yeah, how come you ain't like him?" says Wilfred. "Why you got no tats?"

"I don't know," I say. "We're different."

Antwon says, "Yeah, you different, all right. He's like steel, and you soft like Wonder bread."

"He's almost as soft as Oskar," adds Coty.

But I'm hardly listening.

"Keep ignorin' us," says Antwon. "Just don't be surprised when you get your ass beat."

They all laugh at Antwon's threat, until they lose their focus, shifting to the latest gossip about Oskar.

"Yo, whatever happened to that boy?" says Wilfred.

"He's mental," says Coty.

"I heard he's coming back," says Double X. "He supposed to be better or something."

"He ain't better," says Wilfred. "He mad fucked up. Ain't no pills or doctors nowhere that can fix that shit."

"You remember when that old lady teacher caught him beating it under his desk in her class?" says Coty.

"Yo, that's whack," says Wilfred.

"What's whack is that he beatin' it to her ugly ass," says Double X.

"Yo, there's no choices in here," says Wilfred. "You got to take what you can get!"

They go on, talking about how many *bitches* they've gotten pregnant, the kinds of guns they've carried and shot, and who they will live with when they are released: grandmothers; godmothers; aunts; and uncles fresh out of prison, men they claim are living large in Section Eight apartments in the projects with LCD televisions and white leather furniture.

But my mind is not on them or their stupid stories; it's on Louis and how he used to be my hero. Now I don't want to be like him at all. Not if it means dealing drugs and selling out my friends. And I think that maybe I'm okay with this. He's just my brother now and not my hero. I will not try to be like him. So, then who am I supposed to be like?

I scan Bravo Unit for Samson and Mr. Eboue, but they're not here. Instead Horvath looks back at me, his

155

small hard eyes glinting with meanness and stupidity. He twirls his keys on a lanyard, his fat neck bulging out of his shirt collar, rolls of obscene sweaty skin showing in animal-like contrast to the white cotton of his button-down uniform. Piglike. Bull-like. Ready to teach us his version of manhood. He catches my eyes and sneers at me as if to say that I'm still a slow learner and will need extra lessons.

Blankly, I turn the pages of *The Sea Wolf* and read from a part where Van Weyden and Wolf Larsen are arguing about the value of life. Wolf says:

"I believe that life is a mess. It is like yeast, a ferment, a thing that moves and may move for a minute, an hour, a year, or a hundred years, but that in the end will cease to move. The big eat the little that they may continue to move, the strong eat the weak that they may retain their strength. The lucky eat the most and move the longest, that is all. What do you make of those things?"

It sounds true enough. At least for people like Horvath and Pike; and now my brother. The big eat the little. The strong eat the weak. I know where I stand in this chain, but I don't want to be eaten. I'm tired of being the weak one who gets pushed around. The big question is, when the time comes, how hard will I fight? I don't know, but I go to my room and crank out sets of push-ups and dips until my muscles ache and I can't get up from the floor.

39

Mr. Samson and Mr. E are doing overtime running transport to New York City to pick up a new kid. This means Horvath and Pike are in charge.

"I don't know what Mr. E and Samson usually do for group," says Horvath. "But we're gonna talk about goals, and I don't want to hear any bitching."

Everyone groans. We're sick of talking about goals, because even if we have good ones, realistic ones, it won't matter. Bobby will still be hyperactive and annoying. Antwon will stay lost in the bullshit of his gang. Freddie will keep stealing nice clothes from Bergdorf Goodman. And I will go on being whatever it is that I am supposed to be. The question is, do I get to decide what that something is? I hope so.

Coty mutters, "Forget goals."

"Shut up!" Horvath says. "I told you not to bitch. This isn't a choice. Now, who knows the difference between a real goal and something that's stupid and unrealistic?"

Wilfred raises his hand.

"Go ahead." Pike points at him.

"Getting a job's a real goal," says Wilfred, "but hooking up with a *Hustler* model or going to college is stupid and unrealistic."

Double X says he can get with a *Hustler* model anytime he wants.

"So can I if I pay six bucks at the magazine stand," says Levon. "But that don't count."

Pike shuts the two of them up by standing between their chairs. "Getting a job *is* a realistic goal," he says. "So is going to college."

"No, it ain't," says Wilfred. "Nobody in my family been to college, and I ain't going, either. But I'm gonna work. I know how to fix cars."

"Then that's a good goal," Pike says.

Wilfred beams, proud of his good goal. Then he says, "Mr. Pike, what's your goal?"

I can't tell if the guard is surprised because Wilfred remembered his name, or because someone actually wants to know about his life. He looks at Horvath, who shrugs. "My goal," Pike says slowly, cautiously, "is to get my pilot's license."

Hands shoot up. Questions fly.

"You mean like an airplane?" says Bobby.

"Yes, fly an airplane," says Pike.

"What you have to do to get that kind of license?" says Levon.

"Yo, I want to fly one of them private jets," says Double

X. "With leather seats and a full bar and a hot tub and lots of them *Hustler* girls Wilfred was talking about."

"You fly the plane," Antwon says. "I'll entertain them girls in the hot tub."

Pike silences us with a hand. Despite all the stupid questions, he is smiling for the moment, no longer angry and mean. He seems like a different person, and I wonder if maybe he has needed this all along, a chance to talk about himself and what he wants. Maybe everybody does.

"You need to practice and take a test, and then rack up forty hours of flight time."

"And then what?" I ask. "After you get your license." I'm having trouble picturing him doing anything other than being a guard with Horvath, working the seven-to-three shift. But I want to know, because maybe, if he can have dreams of something else, then I can, too.

"I'm going to retire from this place and work as a pilot."

Horvath gets this sour look on his face. "Come on, Byron," he says. "We're trying to teach these kids about realistic goals, not fantasy."

"This *is* realistic," says Pike.

But Horvath is too bitter and pissed off. He's done listening to whatever Pike or any of us might have to say.

"You ain't getting that license, and everyone knows it. How many years you studied for the airman's test?"

"It's a tough test," Pike says. "There's a written part and then the flight test. It takes a long time to—"

"How many years?" says Horvath.

"Five."

"And how much money you spent on them lessons to get your hours?"

"It ain't about the money, Roy." Pike looks hurt and dejected, just like Wilfred or Bobby when their math assignments come back all marked up with red ink and Mr. Goldschmidt tells them to rewrite it.

"What's it about, then?"

Pike looks around uncertainly. "It's about having something to look forward to," he says.

But Horvath waves it all away with his hand like he's swatting bugs. "Come on, man! In five years you're gonna be right here working doubles with me and Croop. Unless you're too good for that, Mr. Big-Shot Pilot."

You can hear a pin drop, because we have never seen these two turn on each other.

"That ain't a goal," Pike says. "That's just giving up, and I ain't gonna be a lifer. Even if you think it's all I can do."

Horvath sits thinking. His big hands are resting on the knees of his gray work pants, which are stretched tight over his ever-increasing bulk. He looks uncomfortable sitting, like his fat powerful body was made only for working, and the idea of group is more than a waste of time. It's a disgrace, a perversion.

Pike shoots his partner a hard look. "What's your goal, then?" he says. "If you're such an expert."

"I want to coach my son's football team." He says it fast, like he's been waiting a long time for someone to ask, and then he just stares off at the wall, looking deflated. I want to know why he can't coach his son's team, because it sounds like an easy thing to do. Maybe it's because his visitation got cut off, like he said when I first came in to Morton.

After a moment, Pike looks at his watch and says we have to wrap things up. "Real quick," he says, "go around and say what your goal is." Wilfred wants a job at an auto body shop. Levon wants to be a pro ballplayer. Double X is going to be a rap artist or a record producer or a fashion designer. Freddie says he's going to community college, and Coty wants to own a four-wheeler repair shop. Antwon says that he will be a businessman, an entrepreneur.

When it is my turn, my first thought is that I want to help my mother and brother get out of trouble. But I know that's not exactly true anymore. It's not that I don't want to help them; I do. But I don't think they can be helped. I don't think they're going to change.

I close my eyes and imagine Socrates Fortlow saying, "But what do you want for yo'self, boy? What do you want?" And the answer is there, clear in my mind. It's always been there, covered up by layers of fear thick with dust.

"I want to go to college," I say. "I want to live in a dorm where no one will know where I came from or who I was at my old high school. I want to start over and see the world outside of Dunkirk. I want to take writing classes."

Pike seems surprised by my outburst. "Good goal," he says.

Freddie gives me a nod.

"You and Peach can go to college together," says Antwon. "Share a room."

Everyone laughs.

161

"Line up!" says Horvath. "Group's over."

Before I go to sleep, I do sets of twenty-five push-ups. After the fourth set my arms give out and I lie on the floor, exhausted, but happy because I know what I want for myself. I am finally getting strong.

40

Instead of passing by my desk during mail call, Pike drops a letter in front of me. A real letter! It's from Mr. Pfeffer. I can't believe he wrote back. I read it several times, and then ask Mr. Eboue for a piece of tape to put it up on my bedroom wall. It says:

Dear James,

I am so sorry to hear that you are locked up. There are many things that I wish to tell you, chief among them that you are a kind, intelligent, and terrific kid. I believe you'll get out of that place and return to Dunkirk High, where we will toast the occasion with cream soda. (I have changed from root beer in the interest of variety.) You will graduate, and you will make a nice life for yourself. If you can't see this due to your present circumstances, then you must trust me; I know how the story ends, and it's a good ending.

Your friend Samson sounds like a solid man. Stick with him, if you can. I hope you are able to continue to read and write. Remember, voice and perspective! I took the liberty of calling the Morton facility, and was told that only immediate family members may visit. They also told me that I cannot send books, which sounds like a terribly fascist policy, if you ask me. But I will reply promptly to every letter you write. Stay well, and take care of yourself.

Your friend,
Stephen Pfeffer

P.S. Did you finish *The Sea Wolf*? Find anything good within the pages of the story?

41

Response calls ring out on the intercom whenever there's a fight or a restraint. "Team A report to the cafeteria! Team A report to the cafeteria!" The fight could be for something as simple as one kid brushing against another kid's desk in class. The owner of the desk might suck his teeth and return to his work, but later, when no one is looking, words will be exchanged.

"You got a fucking problem, son?" one kid will say.

"Don't call me son, bitch."

The two will stare at each other, puffed-up chests and beating hearts almost touching like opposing forces in perfect but delicate balance. And something will spark, a movement, the twitch of an eye, and then blows will rain down. They will come out of nowhere, loose and wild arms looping in exaggerated arcs. Cracks and soft meaty thumps will filter through the noise of other kids shouting "Get him!" and "Kick his motherfucking ass!" For a moment, the fight will seem unstoppable, the momentum of violence too great for anyone to halt. But the guards always appear in a solid mass of gray uniforms, big men with radios and cuffs and their practiced "physical restraint procedure." The fighting boys' arms will be pinned behind their backs. Levered hip tosses will put them on their faces. The body weight of one or two men will be applied until, either from chest compression or forced submission, the struggle ends.

But today's crisis is something bigger.

"All available staff report to the clinic!" Mr. Pike's radio says. "All available staff, go to the clinic immediately!"

The guards look at each other expectantly. Crupier whispers, "Rivera?"

"I don't know. Maybe," Pike says.

Crupier smiles, excited about the possibility of getting to tangle with the almost famous boxer. He holsters his radio and takes off running, out the door and down the hallway. I watch him join up with a pack of other guards as they hustle toward the clinic.

Mr. Pike looks more irritable than usual, maybe because he's stuck behind on the unit. He will miss the action and have to hear from Horvath and Crupier and the others about how they dropped the great Moses Rivera. He clears his throat and says, "Listen up, ladies. We're on shutdown. So get in your rooms and don't ask no questions, 'cause I don't know what's going on. Now! Move it!"

Some of the boys grumble and suck their teeth, but we go, and the heavy steel doors lock behind us.

I talk to Freddie through the vent for a while, but he doesn't know anything, either.

"Better not be nothing too bad," he says. "'Cause I got my stage, and the last thing I need is some drama to make everyone in here crazy."

I lie down on top of my bed, waiting. I hear the faraway warble of a siren, and if Double X's stories are true, Moses is wreaking havoc on the guards. Secretly I hope he kicks Horvath's ass.

The siren is definitely getting louder, so I put my face against the window and watch the parking lot. A police car and an ambulance pull up. I see a couple of paramedic guys coming through the electric gate, and then, minutes later, they're wheeling somebody out on a hospital gurney. They put the gurney into the back of the ambulance and drive away. Gone.

"You see that?" I ask the heater.

"Yeah," says Freddie.

I spend the next hour pacing and doing push-ups, because I'm sure something really bad has happened; the only question is if it's a kid or a staff member. I go to the heater to ask Freddie what he thinks, but mostly I am freaking out and need someone to talk to. Freddie says he feels it, too, the weird tension in the air, like something terrible has happened, or is happening.

"Could be a riot," Freddie says.

"How do you know?" I say.

"Last time I was here, two boys faked a fight to distract the guards. Then the others who was in on it fucked up someone else. They punched him in the face so many times that he got knocked out and had a broken cheekbone."

"Why did they do it?"

"'Cause he squealed on another kid, that's why. Don't do that. No matter what."

He takes my silence to mean that I'm not convinced. "I ain't lying," he says. "Only thing lower than S.O.'s is kids who rat out other kids." *S.O.* stands for "sex offender," which is what the guards call kids who have molested other kids.

At nine o'clock we're let out of our bedrooms one by one to use the toilet and get ready for bed.

"What about showers?" Levon says.

I expect Pike to bark or shout, but all he says is "Tomorrow" in a voice so quiet and sad that I have to look twice to make sure it's him. He doesn't even bitch when it takes us twice as long as it should to wash up. Back in my room I sit all night by my door, looking out the small rectangular window. Pike is at his station in a plastic chair with his elbows on his knees, rocking gently back and forth. Aside from picking up the phone a couple of times, he doesn't get out of the chair. I pass this information to Freddie, who isn't able to see from the angle of his door window.

"Keep watching," he says. "Something bad is going down, and I wanna know what it is."

"I'll watch," I say, knowing full well that neither of us will sleep a wink tonight.

At midnight Crupier, Pike, and Mr. Eboue burst into the staff office. They are talking and gesturing wildly, but I can't hear what they're saying because the door connecting the office to the unit floor is closed. I'm not sure, but it looks like Crupier is crying. His face is red, and he keeps swiping at his eyes. Mr. Eboue puts a hand on his shoulder, but Crupier pulls away and shoves open the door to the main hallway.

When I tell Freddie, he says, "Shit. Somebody dead."

42

The remaining guards stay in the staff office, talking through the rest of the night. At wake-up, all three of them, Pike, Horvath, and Eboue, unlock our rooms and gather us in the dayroom.

Mr. E says, "How many of you remember Oskar? Raise your hands."

It's all of us except for Kyle, who arrived after Tony left. Kyle's from Syracuse and has the worst acne I've ever seen. He's quiet but supposedly shot another kid in a robbery.

"I'm sorry to tell you this, but Oskar passed away last night."

There's a moment of dull faces and silence.

"Where was he?" Wilfred asks.

"Right here," says Mr. Pike. "At Morton. He got back from the hospital last week."

"How'd he die?" says Levon.

"Suicide," says Mr. Eboue. "He hanged himself. That's private information, but I'm telling you this because you knew him, and because you'll hear about it anyway. You deserve to know right away, and to hear it from one of us."

The rest of the morning is quiet and serious, but the other guys eat everything on their plates at breakfast: chocolate chip muffins, small boxes of Frosted Flakes cereal, and Eggo waffles with butter and syrup. Freddie, who has the strangest eating habits of anyone on the unit, sprinkles his waffles with a fried egg and Frosted Flakes. Then he rolls it and stuffs the thing into his mouth. Levon, who is surprisingly proper about table manners and the overall cleanliness of the unit, shakes his head in disgust.

I peel back the foil on two small syrup packages and drip the syrup into each individual square of my Eggos. But when I'm done, I can't eat, because I've got this image stuck in my head of Oskar hanging in his room from a shoelace or a bedsheet. In my head, I see his body slowly twisting around. When he turns enough to face me, I look right into those big vacant eyes. And what's really freaky is that I can't tell if he's dead, because it's the same expression he had the last time I saw him in the gym, just after he sank that shot with the basketball.

After breakfast Wilfred asks if we're going to have a funeral.

"No funeral here," Mr. Pike says. "His family will have one for him."

Already Wilfred's hand is stretching up to the ceiling, ready for the next question.

"What?" Pike says, getting a little pissed off. Strangely, his irritability is comforting, as though things might be returning to normal.

"Then how are we s'posed to say goodbye?"

Pike sighs. "I don't know, Wilfred. Maybe ask the chaplain if you go to church this Sunday."

"Okay," Wilfred says, apparently satisfied.

The whole question of a funeral makes me think of the scene in *The Sea Wolf* when Wolf Larsen's first mate drinks himself to death. After cursing and kicking the dead body (for leaving the ship shorthanded at the beginning of a voyage), the Wolf orders the corpse to be sewn up in some scrap canvas along with a sack of coal (for weight, to pull the body down to the bottom of the sea). Nobody on board the *Ghost* has a Bible, so the Wolf says:

"I only remember one part of the service, . . . and that is, 'And the body shall be cast into the sea.' So cast it in."

And then Van Weyden says, "The cruelty of the sea, its relentlessness and awfulness, rushed upon me. Life had become cheap and tawdry, a beastly and inarticulate thing, a soulless stirring of the ooze and slime."

That's how it feels right now. Oskar's dead, and all that's left is a pile of kids' books. *Cheap and tawdry.* I don't know what we could do to make it seem better. Maybe have a service. We should at least try.

Later, I see people from the state walking around the facility to investigate. They wear suits, with ID badges hanging around their necks, and they smile politely. In class Ms. Bonetta tries to talk to us about Oskar. She says that every suicide is preventable, if only we can notice the signs. But then she gets too teary to continue and excuses herself. Pike takes over and puts on a video of *The Outsiders,* which is an old movie that I think is based on a book. It's really good, and soon I'm happy to be lost in the struggles of Ponyboy and Johnny, instead of thinking about Oskar and my own problems. But then the two boys rescue some kids from a burning church, and Johnny gets his back broken by a giant timber. He's taken to a hospital and declared a hero, but then he dies! I wasn't expecting him to die, and maybe it's because of what just happened to Oskar, but I feel like I'm going to freak out.

"Sit down, James," Mr. Pike shouts.

I find myself standing up at my desk, breathing fast, eyes stinging with the beginnings of tears. Because of what just happened to Johnny, and how unfair it is. I sit down, but I really want to cry out, or scream, or hit something. I don't understand why he had to die. Is it because he was kind and tried to help those kids? Is that the message? It must be, because at the end of the movie this guy, Dally, who's a friend of Ponyboy's, says, "You'd better wise up, Pony . . . you get tough like me and you don't get hurt. You look out for yourself and nothin' can touch you. . . ."

It's a really intense, crazy scene, and you just know Dally's going to do something really stupid because he can't accept that someone as nice and good as Johnny can die. And sure enough, in one of the final scenes, he points an empty gun at the cops. I forgot about the other boys in the room with me, and now they're all shouting out at the cops.

"Don't shoot!" says Wilfred. "He's just bugging out 'cause his friend died!"

"He ain't got no bullets!" says Double X.

But the cops don't listen. And in a way, Dally is committing suicide—because he knew this was going to happen.

He wanted it. All of which makes me think again about Oskar. He wanted to die, too, and I didn't even really know him. I don't think anybody did. How are you supposed to *know* someone who stares at his hands all day, and cracks his head open on a concrete wall? I think the other boys are just as confused, because, with the exception of a few meaningless comments like, "Damn!" and "That sucks," they, too, have had nothing to say about Oskar's death.

I should probably feel something more about his death, but I don't. It's messed up that he killed himself, and it's messed up that the guards broke Bobby's arm. And it's not right, either, that we have to spend months in a place where no one is getting any better. No one is learning anything, as far as I can see. In some ways, it seems like people are getting worse. Am I? I don't think so, but who knows.

What's most surprising to me about Oskar's death is how upset the guards appear. From the day-to-day stuff, you'd think that most of them hate us. Except for Samson and Eboue, they call us names and tell us that we're never going to amount to anything. They laugh at us and humiliate us practically every day.

But now they seem somber and thoughtful, like it's a huge tragedy and every one of our miserable lives is precious. Even Horvath has been quiet and sad-looking. He's got dark circles under his eyes, and greasy stuck-down hair, like he's been up for days without showering. He still sucks coffee from his giant beer keg of a thermos, but there are no bags of fast food from McDonald's, Taco Bell, Wendy's, or Subway. He hasn't even joked around with the other guards, his typical mean remarks replaced by grunts and a far-off stare.

Crupier hasn't returned to work, and I heard that he was the one who had to cut Oskar down. Apparently Oskar had ripped out a cord or piece of piping from the side of a mattress and strung himself up with it from a light fixture in the ceiling.

At lights-out, I can't sleep. I do a hundred push-ups and squats at a time, but after, I still see Oskar turning around and around on his mattress cord, his rhyming picture books scattered on the floor beneath him. I pull out *The Sea Wolf* and read the part about the burial at sea, which gives me an idea. I call out to Freddie through the heater vent. "I want to do a funeral service for Oskar."

Freddie says, "Okay. Just tell me what to do."

"Repeat after me. *'And the body shall be cast into the sea.'*"

He says, *"And the body shall be cast into the sea."*

"I'm sorry you died, Oskar," I say. "I didn't know you, but I hope you find peace."

"Amen," says Freddie.

I continue reading out loud:

"*'They elevated the end of the hatch-cover with pitiful haste, and, like a dog flung overside, the dead man slid feet first into the sea. The coal at his feet dragged him down. He was gone . . . the dead man, dying obscenely, buried sordidly, and sinking down, down . . . And this strange vessel, with its terrible men, pressed under by wind and sea and ever leaping up and out, was heading away into the south-west, into the great and lonely Pacific expanse.'*"

43

Dear Mr. Pfeffer,

Thank you for writing back to me. I really appreciate it, because no one else writes, and also because you are someone I respect. You've taught me a lot through the books you've given me, even if it's hard to show what I've learned in real life. I think the reason for this is because Morton is a bad place where everyone is stressed and on each other's last nerve. One boy got his arm broken by the guards for nothing. Another boy killed himself. I hardly knew him, but I think he was crazy. His name was Oskar.

Another reason why it's hard to show what I've learned is because I am about as out of place here as Van Weyden was on the *Ghost*. All of the boys are tough and ready to fight. And there's a guard,

Horvath, who's like Wolf Larsen, except not as smart.

There are so many parallels (between my life right now and that book) that it seems too much for coincidence, like you gave it to me to prepare. I know that's not possible, but I won't deny that I skipped ahead to the end. I figured that if Van Weyden made it, if he was able to stand up to Wolf Larsen and live, then I'd be okay, too. But then I learned that almost everyone on the ship dies! And Van Weyden survives only because Wolf Larsen has a stroke, which seems too convenient, like Jack London didn't end it the way it's really supposed to, with one of them killing the other. And this (realizing how it *should* end) worries me, especially if Horvath is *my* Wolf Larsen. What a twisted thought! I hope to God it's not true.

Anyway, it's my new favorite book, and I'm pretty sure I've found one of the secrets you mentioned. It's in an exchange between Van Weyden and Wolf Larsen on page 177:

Van Weyden: "You will observe there," I said, "a slight trembling. It is because I am afraid, the flesh is afraid; and I am afraid in my mind because I do not wish to die. But my spirit masters the trembling flesh and the qualms of the mind. I am more than brave. I am courageous. Your flesh is not afraid. You are not afraid. On the one hand, it costs you nothing to encounter danger; on the other hand, it even gives you delight. You enjoy it. You may be unafraid, Mr. Larsen, but you must grant that the bravery is mine."

Wolf Larsen: "You're right," he acknowledged at once. "I never thought of it in that way before. But is the opposite true? If you are braver than I, am I more cowardly than you?"

At first I didn't think this passage applied to me. I thought that if I kept to myself and didn't cause any trouble, I'd be okay. But I'm starting to believe that it's not possible to avoid trouble at Morton, just like it wasn't possible for Van Weyden on the *Ghost*. He had to get a knife and prepare to fight the cook, even though he was terrified. He had soft hands, but he still had to learn how to splice rope, set sails, and navigate. And I am learning things, too. That guy I told you about, Samson? He's teaching me to lift weights, and I'm getting really strong. And my brother, Louis? Let's just say that I won't be following in his footsteps anymore. I guess I'll have to make my own path from now on.

Write back again, if you can.

Sincerely,
James

44

After a week, nobody talks about Oskar anymore and things start to get back to normal. At the Ping-Pong table some of the guys bring up Moses Rivera.

"When do you think he's coming?" says Wilfred.

"Don't talk about him no more," Double X says.

"Why not?" says Wilfred, indignant. "Moses is the bomb."

"Because, my mother goes to the same church with Moses's godmother. She say something happened to him."

"Then he ain't coming here?"

"No, he ain't coming here."

Double X drops his paddle on the table and walks away.

"What's his problem?" says Wilfred.

"Nothing," Coty says. "Xavier ain't got a problem, but Moses do. Some dude stabbed him in a fight. He's alive, but no more boxing."

Nobody has much to say until after school, when we have group. Mr. E begins by asking again for a show of hands. "I know it's been a few weeks, but who remembers that scenario I gave you, about the punk who stepped on your new Jordans and didn't apologize or show any respect?"

Arms shoot up straight and high.

"James?" he says. "How would you respond?"

I can feel everyone's eyes on me. Aside from Antwon, who is too cool and hard-core for the group, I'm the quietest.

"What's your answer?"

I look around. Antwon is picking at his nails, playing indifferent. Levon stares out the window. The other guys and Mr. E look at me, waiting. "If it's bad for my family," I say, "I won't fight."

Freddie nods, but the gang kids mutter. Antwon calls me a pussy, and Levon says that I'm not making a choice, because I don't know how to fight anyway.

But Mr. E gives me a thumbs-up and speaks to the group. "This here scenario is a choice. Stay with your family, or fight and get locked up. Love on the one hand, hate on the other. Which do you stand for? Which do you believe in?"

He looks around the circle at us, one at a time, his dark eyes working their way into ours like he can see inside and know what we're made of. I know what I'm made of, but I wonder about these other guys. What's inside of Antwon? Double X? Or Freddie, for that matter? I know they're as screwed up as I am on the surface, but what's way down deep, beneath all the attitude and talk—something really strong, or the same thin bullshit that made Louis set me up? I want to know what the right way to be is. Why can't Mr. E tell me that?

Mr. E pulls out a stack of index cards and a box of sharpened pencils. He hands them out while Samson counts to make sure we don't steal them for weapons.

"What do you want us to do with these?" Wilfred says.

"I want you to write down your choice. Put your name on it if you want."

We turn the blank cards over in our hands.

"Eighty-six percent of the boys who leave this place will get rearrested," says Mr. Eboue. "That means only fourteen percent will make it. The choice you put on this card will determine which one you will be."

"What happens to the cards?" says Coty.

"Your card will stay on the bulletin board until you leave. Then you take it with you."

"Why we gotta take it with us?"

"So you'll know which one you are. So there'll be no surprises."

We sit around, uncertain, confused.

"Go ahead," Mr. E says. "Choose."

Slowly, reluctantly, we write down our choices. I know I'm not going to get arrested again, so it's not much of a choice for me. I am going back to high school, where I will take every class that Mr. Pfeffer teaches. And I'm going to read all kinds of good books and study hard so I can get into college and leave Dunkirk. That's what I'm going to do.

The other kids are scrunching up their faces from the

effort; for them, it's a very hard decision. Mr. Samson collects our cards and looks them over. "I'm going to read them out loud, but I'm saying right now, you guys need to work on your spelling."

We laugh, nervous about our words being read aloud. Group is the one place where we're allowed to talk about our past lives; the rest of the time, guards tell us to shut up and mind our own business.

"Okay," says Samson. "The first card says, *'I'll fight.'*

"Second card: *'I will stay and help my family.'*

"Third card says: *'Fight.'*

"Next card: *'The right answer is to walk away, but I ain't weak. I've seen what happens to weak people.'*

"Let's talk about this," Samson says. "What happens to weak people?"

Shouts ring out, until Samson raises his hand and points to it as a reminder.

Levon raises his hand first. "If you're weak," he begins, scrunching up his face like he's trying to force out the right words, "girls don't want to be with you. And your little brothers and little cousins won't look up to you. If you're weak, nobody want to be your friend."

"You all agree?" Samson says, scanning our faces quickly. "How about being kind to other people?" he says.

"Same thing," says Levon. "People mistake your kindness for weakness."

"Yeah," Coty says. "You kind, you weak." Samson says we're almost out of time, but he wants to talk more about this. He quickly reads the rest of the cards and tapes them up on the bulletin board.

"Now," he says, "you all need to stand by your choices. Fighters should expect to get locked up again. If you can accept that, then there's no shame in it. Everybody is free to do whatever they want in life, so long as they accept the cost."

Coty raises his hand and waits to be called on. "But, Mr. Samson, what if I change my mind?"

Mr. Samson smiles. "Then you get a new card." He holds one out.

Coty thinks about it, then looks at Antwon and Double X. "Not yet," he says.

Back in my room, I pull out my Jack London book and read Wolf Larsen's take on the whole argument:

"Might is right, and that is all there is to it. Weakness is wrong. Which is a very poor way of saying that it is good for oneself to be strong, and evil for oneself to be weak—or better yet, it is pleasurable to be strong, because of the profits; painful to be weak, because of the penalties."

45

It's hard to believe I've been here for almost three months. My old life in Dunkirk seems far away, and what I really want is to go out in my old hooded sweatshirt and walk. I want to eat breakfast at Rusty's Diner, and then joke around with Earl, the janitor. I want to sit in school and listen to Mr. Pfeffer tell stories and talk about books. But my sweatshirt is locked up in Central Services, along with everyone else's street clothes. I'll have to wait at least three more months before I can put it on and walk out of here (and that's if I can get early release, which seems like this mysterious thing that so far only Tony has gotten).

There are no more good books to read, either. After finishing *The Sea Wolf* and *Always Outnumbered, Always Outgunned*, I tried reading the stack of paperback thrillers and mysteries on the Bravo bookshelf. But after the second one, they all seemed the same. Out of boredom I pull out the big unabridged dictionary, a musty leather-bound thing that must weigh twenty pounds. I flip absently through the onionskin pages.

"We got to talk, dawg," says Antwon from behind me. "Ain't nobody gonna interrupt, either, so sit your ass down."

"Okay."

He sits a little too close, eyeballing me. I look back at him. The tension reminds me of a *Sea Wolf* chapter where Van Weyden and the cook sit at opposite ends of the galley, sharpening their knives on whetstones. "Whet, whet, whet, it went all day long. The look in his eyes as he felt the keen edge and glared at me was positively carnivorous."

Antwon doesn't exactly look carnivorous, but he's sure not friendly.

"Me and Coty and Double X been talking," he says. "We decided to hold off on giving you a beat-down. Instead we gonna give you a chance to prove yourself. A opportunity."

"No offense, but I don't want any opportunities. I just want to do my program and get out."

"I hear that, but me and my boys, we got this plan, see, and we want you to be in on it."

He slides down in his chair, all relaxation and confidence. His long legs are splayed out in front of him, hands dangling off the armrests, bony knuckles crosshatched with scars. I try to think of what Louis would do. He would probably bring the dictionary down right on his kneecap. Antwon wouldn't even see it coming. And then what? Louis would smash an elbow into his face. He'd say something like, "That's what I think of your opportunity, fuckhead." But I can't see myself doing that. I'm not Louis or Wolf Larsen. I'm more like Van Weyden. The run-and-hide type.

185

"Why me?" I say.

"Because, man, you're all on your own. Like me and Coty and Double X. None of us are going anywhere for a long time, unless we take things into our own hands, which is what we're talking about doing. You down?"

"I don't know," I say.

Antwon sits up in his chair and opens his eyes all the way. They are brown and empty, like there's no real person inside him, just a tall skinny kid with scarred knuckles who cares only about his reputation and the power of his gang.

"Yeah, you do," he says. "You either in or you out, so don't be like your faggot friend, Freddie. Be a man and make up your own mind."

I ignore the comment about Freddie. What would I do about it anyway? Nothing.

"Why would you even want me? I don't know anything about gangs," I say, trying to talk my way out. "I'd probably mess things up."

"Don't worry about that. My crew got plans for your pasty ass. And right now we can use you."

"I have to think about it."

"You're disappointing me, man. Why you wanna do that?" He nudges my canvas sneaker with his own, down low where no guards can see. "Tell you what. Offer's good for three days, then we ask someone else and you out."

He holds up his fist for a bump even though the guards will notice and yell.

"Later, white bread."

I touch his fist cautiously like it might be a trick, like

it might explode in my face, but nothing happens. The guards are not watching.

At night I knock three times on the heater and tell Freddie about my conversation. I ask him what kind of a plan he thinks Antwon is working on.

"I don't know," he says. "Those three assholes couldn't escape from a paper bag. It's probably something stupid like beating up another kid; that's what it usually is. You just need to keep away from him, James. He's shady and shifty, times ten. Know what he did to get in here?"

"What?" I'm listening, but I don't really want to hear. Why can't I just do my program and leave? Why can't I keep to myself and be invisible? I wish I was back at home, where I was invisible, wandering the streets and neighborhoods in my shitty sweatshirt and holey sneakers.

Sometimes I think that the world won't allow people like me, like it's going to stamp out and crush everyone who is weak and mild. Because even though I'm getting physically tougher, I'm not a fighter, and I don't know what I'll do when things come to a head with Antwon. Is it wrong to find your way without fighting or taking from other people? It must be.

"He beat some dude with a piece of pipe," Freddie says. "Dude was lost and asked for directions. Antwon was with his boys and said, 'I'm gonna help this poor brother find his way.' Dude got a cracked skull and lost an eye."

I shouldn't be surprised, but I am.

46

After several weeks of working out with Samson, I am finally changing, getting stronger and visibly bigger. Tonight he comes on shift and takes Freddie and me to the weight room for Stage Night. It's become a ritual: one hour of lifting followed by take-out food.

I go through the warm-ups he showed me, while Freddie heads straight for the stair climber. He rotates the TV set on its wall mount so he can watch a gossip show that Horvath has prohibited on Bravo Unit, with the declaration, "No queer shit on my unit."

When I'm done stretching and warming up, Samson loads the bar on the bench press with twenty-five-pound plates.

"I want fifteen," he says.

I space my hands out on the bar, shoulder width, like he showed me. I breathe deep, repeat, and then lift the bar on the third exhalation. The reps come off easy, and for the first time I feel truly powerful, like I can do anything.

On the last rep Samson guides the bar up and says, "Good. Now rest for thirty seconds."

I sit on the bench, breathing, my head perfectly clear for the first time in days. No thoughts of Louis and my mother. No images of Oskar twisting on his home-made mattress-cover noose above a pile of his little-kid books.

Samson says, "You're a lot stronger than you know."

I can't help smiling, a weird feeling of heat spreading out over my body that might be happiness. I look over at Freddie sweating and dancing and pumping his legs, which are surprisingly skinny for a chunky guy like him. The TV spews some crap about how to get your house ready for a big dinner party. Samson replaces the twenty-five-pound plates with forty-fives, and then adds a ten to each side, bringing the weight, including the forty-five-pound bar, up to 155 pounds. He thumps me on my shoulder and says, "Give me three good ones."

I push out the set nice and smooth, controlling the weight. "I can do more," I say after racking up the bar.

"I know. But we're tricking your muscles. If they know what's coming next, they'll never grow. You won't get stronger."

He pulls the two small plates off, bringing the weight back down to 135. "No rest," he says. "Give me twelve quick ones."

I get to ten before my arms start to burn and tremble. "Come on," says Samson. I grit my teeth and push out the last two. He adds a twenty-five-pound plate on each side. "Now I want one strong one," he says after I've had a longer rest.

I grip the bar and take my deep breaths. I lift the weight off the rack, excited that I might be able to do it. But when I lower the bar, my muscles give out and I am stuck with 185 pounds resting on my chest. I grunt and push, but it doesn't move.

"You got this," Samson says, bending down, putting the tips of his index fingers under the bar. "Push it out!"

I drive my heels into the floor like he taught me and push even harder. Incredibly, like magic, the bar goes up. Slowly. Steadily. It's got to be Samson, but how can someone lift so much with his fingers?

"One more," he says at the top. My arms are shaking like crazy, like they're put together with rubber bands. I lower the bar.

"Now push it up!" he says, before I drop it all the way to my chest. "Show me you want this!" He's hovering over my face, encouraging, shouting.

Again the bar starts to rise slowly, like it's being propelled by the power of Samson's words. At the top he racks it, says, "Nice job, man. You did it!" He is grinning, happy, though I don't know why. I'd have been crushed if he hadn't helped.

"Thanks," I say.

"Don't thank me. That was all you." He pulls a water bottle from his duffel bag and hands it to me. "Drink this. It'll help you recover."

It tastes terrible, like chalk mixed with powdered milk. "That was not *all me*," I say. "I couldn't do it."

"You *did*," he says. "It's a mind trick. Your brain tells you I'm helping, but I'm really not. I hardly touched the bar."

I finish up with fifteen repetitions at the starting weight. It feels light, like nothing at all, but my arms are beyond spent, and it's like I'm pushing with someone else's dead limbs. Samson helps me with the last two, and then gives me the bottle of chalky milk again.

During squats he says, "There's a difference between getting big and becoming strong. To get big, you hit it hard and go heavy, over and over again until it doesn't feel heavy anymore. Or you can take the juice. Or you can shave your head and get tattoos, rip the sleeves off your shirt and buy a Harley. But none of that is real strength."

Freddie stops climbing his machine and falls like a puddle to the floor. "What's real strength, Samson?" he says.

"It's when you're a balanced man. When you can think as well as you can use your body. And you have to know who you are and be okay with it. If that means that you're not ripped or tough or a badass, then so be it," says Samson.

"But the most important part," he says, "is that you have to believe in something that is real and true. A lot of guys don't believe in anything. They will tell you what they are against, what they don't like, but they can't tell you what they are for. Because they don't actually believe in anything."

I say, "What do *you* believe in?"

It's too personal a question, but I really want to know. I've been waiting a long time to have this conversation.

"I believe in people," he says. "Good people like my family and my friends." After a moment he adds, "And I believe in you, James. Because you trusted me to teach you something, and today your skinny ass lifted a lot of plates. And that impresses the hell out of me. Now let's go eat."

47

At breakfast I am still glowing from Samson's compliment. "I believe in you, James," he had said. My arms,
shoulders, and chest burn with the memory of what I did
in the weight room. One hundred and eighty-five pounds!
Maybe I'll call Louis and tell him, even if he's an asshole
and might not care. But from now on, that's his business—
whether or not he cares. I can still brag if I feel like it.

Antwon's eyes stay fixed on me all day to let me know
that he's not going to forget about his *offer*. One more day
left. Freddie says that there's no plan and Antwon's just
fucking with me, seeing how far he can push until I snap.
He whispers that I should kick him in his knee when we're
in the lunch line. He points at his own leg and says, "Get
him right here on the side; it'll buckle. Then you take his
fuckin' head and smash it on the metal counter. You do
that, and he won't mess with you no more. I guarantee it."

At our table Antwon eats his food and buses his tray.
Then he sits quietly, pretending to mind his own business,
while secretly eyeballing me every time Horvath dips his

own head to shovel up his macaroni and cheese. When the guard goes up to get a second helping, Antwon says, "You in?"

I shrug.

"Go on and shrug," he says. "See what happens to your bitch ass."

There are rumors that Pike is coming in later with a new resident. I wonder who it is and if he will look as scared as I did. But all my curiosity disappears when Pike comes in with a kid who looks a lot like Tony, only a little older and with a hard, mean face instead of Tony's perpetual wiseass grin. He is carrying a stack of state-issued clothes and a yellow resident handbook. He stares straight ahead, avoiding our eyes.

Even when Pike says to the boy, "Tony, take room number one," I still don't want to believe it's him. How could it be? Tony was smart. He knew how to take care of himself. But the really dark thought is, *If he can't make it, then what chance is there for the rest of us?*

Tony goes into room number one and starts putting away his clothes. Mr. Pike shuts the door to give him some space. It's an uncharacteristically kind gesture, but he follows it up with something rude.

"Mr. Honors Stage, my ass." He says it loudly enough for everyone to hear, especially Levon, who is Tony's enemy from their old neighborhood. Supposedly they were in rival gangs, although every gang seems to be the rival of every other gang.

Suddenly Levon is happy and full of life. "Permission to ask a question, sir?" he says to Mr. Pike.

"What?" Pike says.

"Can I, like, welcome Tony back to Bravo Unit?"

"Shut up, Levon," says Pike. "You'll be back here again, too, so don't get all high-and-mighty."

Levon scowls, which is to say that he goes back to being himself.

Tony stays in his room for hours, and it is not until dinnertime, when Mr. E and Samson are supervising us, that he tells Freddie, Wilfred, and me what happened.

"Everything was going good," he says. "I got a job at El Taino Café and I was getting it from my girl every single night. I swear!"

Everyone smiles in appreciation of easy sex.

"You get busted for weed?" Wilfred asks.

"Man, I hardly smoked at all, and I was careful."

"That's good," says Wilfred.

"So what happened?" Freddie says.

"My girl told me she was pregnant. And she's religious and shit, so she wanted to, you know, keep it. And I wanted to be a real man and be responsible and shit, so I said, 'Fuck it, let's have a baby.'"

Usually we aren't allowed to have real conversations in the cafeteria. Whenever Horvath or Pike or Crupier works, it is strictly eat and run. But Mr. E and Samson tell us that the only way to learn how to have normal conversations that aren't focused on drugs and gangs is to practice. So Mr. E just breezes by to make sure we're not plotting a revolt or something, and then he touches Tony on the shoulder and says, "It's good that you're telling your story, Tony. There's no shame in making mistakes, so long as you're man enough to learn something from them. Right, guys?"

"Yes," we all say, dying to hear the end of the story. Any news of the outside world, even bad news, is welcome, and Tony's story promises to be good.

He continues. "So I was all set to pick up more hours at El Taino, when I start thinking about time and shit."

"What do you mean?" Wilfred says, looking at the clock for clues.

"Like, how long does it take for a girl to *really* know she's pregnant?"

"Damn!"

"Damn is right," Tony says. "Long story short, I found out some dude was taking my place with her while I was locked up."

"Who was it?"

"Man, it don't matter who it was. What matters is I took care of his stupid ass."

"And your girlfriend?"

"She ain't my girlfriend no more."

"So what now?" I ask.

"I don't know," he says. "But there's no way I'm doing another year in this place without no privileges. I can tell you that much. They gonna have to send me somewhere else. I'll see to that."

Back at the unit, someone has slipped a note into my school folder. It says, "Times up. Mak yore desishun."

It takes me a minute to figure out the last word, but I have no doubt who it's from or what it means.

48

After lunch Mr. Pike drops an envelope onto my desk. It's from Mr. Pfeffer:

Dear James,

I am sorry to hear about the terrible events at Morton. I am filled with stupid adult questions. How can such things happen in a state facility? Aren't there investigators or people to step in and make changes? Like I said, stupid questions. Because I can tell from your letter that you are experiencing a reality that might be difficult for the rest of us to comprehend. We don't want to know that ours is a world that isn't safe and doesn't always make sense. I hope only that you get out soon and with as much dignity as possible.

Good job finding that passage in *The Sea Wolf*. It's important, I think, to know that a man can be afraid and that this doesn't necessarily diminish him. I have been in places where it was necessary to be afraid (Laos and Vietnam). The only people not to show fear were crazy.

I sincerely hope for your sake that there is no Wolf Larsen at Morton. I have known only one such person in my time, and all I can suggest is to stay clear. You cannot reason with or fight a man like this. He will destroy anyone in his way. Accordingly, I agree with your observation that the ending of *The Sea Wolf* did not fit the story or Larsen's character. A fight to the death did seem imminent, and appropriate.

I like what you said about finding your own path. I hope you'll forgive me for taking the liberty, but after I read your last letter, I went and signed you up for my Advanced Placement English 11 class. We'll be reading a bunch of books I think you'll enjoy, and the class can benefit from your voice and perspective. You can start at the beginning of next semester, or whenever you get back. (It's all squared away with your guidance counselor.)

Take care, James. Keep reading, thinking, and writing.

Your friend,
Stephen Pfeffer

49

Time is up on Antwon's offer. All day throughout class I hear him and his boys whispering, calling me pussy, and punk-ass. I try to ignore it, but I can't. My chest feels tight and I start to sweat. I'm so sick of taking shit from people like Antwon. I don't want to take any more shit.

Antwon sees me standing in the dayroom waiting for him. He lopes over. "Yo," he says. "Time's up. You in?"

"No," I say flatly. My eyes narrow. My breathing gets shallow.

"No's for pussies and faggots. Which one are you?"

I look around at the bloodthirsty faces of Levon, Double X, and Wilfred. They are hungry for violence. They want something exciting to happen, something to take their minds off the day-to-day of school, chores, and getting bossed around by guards who hate them.

"Come on, man, tell us! Which are you?" Coty and Double X join in.

I want to ask them why there aren't other choices.

Because if all you can be is either a pussy or a faggot, or someone like Antwon, who is strong but empty, then I think we're all doomed. Wolf Larsen, with all of his strength, ended up being pathetic and alone. And dead. Socrates, too. His fists, his rock breakers, only brought him pain. It wasn't until he started thinking, and questioning, that he found any peace.

Antwon steps closer. "I asked you a question. Are you a pussy, or a faggot?"

"Neither," I say, scanning the unit floor for guards. I see Horvath in the staff office talking on the phone; Pike is nowhere to be seen.

"Prove it," he says, and shoots a sticky glob of snot onto my chest. I look down at it passively, a greenish-yellow slimy thing stuck to my red shirt. I take in the ring of boys, their animal faces hard and crazy. They are urging me to lose control and fight. And again something is changing inside me, because I *do* feel like losing control. I *do* feel like fighting. The muscles in my arms and chest flex and tighten, ready for action. It's a new feeling, and for the first time in my life I think I could really hurt someone. It's like the glob of snot is made of concentrated hate and it is burning through my clothes, seeping into my skin, contaminating me with rage. I want to wash it off before it consumes me and I do something stupid, something bad that will cost me my stage and keep me here longer. But maybe none of that matters anymore. Maybe all that matters is that I finally act. The boys seem to sense my readiness. They can tell that the fight is welling up in me, trying to take shape and get out. They all jeer. Cajole. Call names.

On its own, without any thinking or planning, my body lunges. My legs coil and spring and I am airborne, driving through space toward Antwon's stupid grinning face. His expression shows surprise as I close my fingers around his throat, thumbs digging and squeezing at the soft spots on the sides of his windpipe, my body and hands possessing their own ugly knowledge.

We crash over a desk and onto the floor. Antwon makes a whomping noise as the impact knocks the air out of him. He tries to breathe, but my fingers press harder and shut off his supply. I am staring into his eyes, which roll back and forth with panic. What is he looking for—someone to help him? He should know that nobody's gonna help him. He should know that it's just him and me now, and it's like Wolf Larsen said: "The big eat the little that they may continue to move, the strong eat the weak that they may retain their strength. The lucky eat the most and move the longest, that is all."

Antwon thrashes his body and claws at my face, but still, my hands hold firm. I am not letting go.

I could kill him, I think. *I could do it. And he knows it.*

Someone pounds me on the back and calls my name.

"James!" Freddie says. "Don't do it. Let him go!" He tries to pull me off, but the other boys pull him away, hard.

"Leave 'em alone!" they say.

I release my grip; Antwon gasps for breath. He sucks air in violent spasms, chest heaving and expanding to get more, in case my fingers threaten to squeeze again. But they don't, and Antwon takes the opportunity to drive his knee up and into my balls. The pain explodes, knocking me clean off him and onto my side. And from this position I watch his white canvas sneaker connect with my face, before the world turns fuzzy and then black.

50

I come out of my first real fight with a knot on my head, a pair of seriously swollen nuts, and no more stage privileges—which means that I won't get to lift weights with Samson anymore. Antwon, who had no privileges to lose, got another month added on to his sentence.

The facility doctor, an Indian man with small dark hands, checked me out and said I was basically fine. He said I could even play in the big flag football game Horvath and Pike have been planning all week. The game is seven on seven on the outside field with these Velcro belts that have a red flag on each hip. It's a big deal for Bravo Unit, something that they only do once each year. Everyone except Freddie has been excited, and even though it's been raining nonstop for three days and the field is thick with mud, the guys can't wait to get out there to play. I've decided to play, too, even though my balls hurt when I run.

Only a couple of the guys are real athletes, like Levon, who played on his high school football team in Queens. And Double X can slam-dunk a basketball, and run faster than anyone else on the unit. Tony is good, too, though Horvath says he's got lousy technique and gets by mostly on strength. I am a terrible athlete, but I like being outside. Even though we are surrounded by a razor wire fence, I can close my eyes and feel the wind and rain and pretend that I am back home at the river, watching fly fishermen or reading a book on a flat sun-warmed rock.

Freddie is the only one who isn't interested in the game, and he complains bitterly. "No way," he says to nobody in particular. "I ain't going in that mud."

I tell him to shut up, but he doesn't listen. I remind him that he could get written up and lose his stage, but he keeps on bitching.

"Put my ass in medical," he says. "I'll even do extra chores."

Horvath walks by grinning, a sack of red and yellow pinnies slung over his shoulder. Normally he'd write Freddie up or at least give him a hard time. Instead he says, "What's the matter, Peach? Afraid you're going to get your clit dirty?"

The unit explodes with laughter, myself included. I don't know why I'm laughing, because I am supposed to be Freddie's friend. And also it's a stupid joke. But I really *do* want to play football in the mud, like a regular kid, and I'm sick and tired of all the fights and arguments. It's like I am too tired to resist anymore, too tired to stand up for Freddie against Horvath and Pike, and against the other boys, who are so quick to laugh at the gay jokes or the dick jokes or, in this case, the dirty clit jokes. Freddie tries his best to laugh it off, but I can see that he is tired of it, too, but in different ways. Tired of being laughed at and picked on. Tired of never being taken seriously, even when he is the only one with a plan and a ticket to college.

Outside, Freddie and I put on red pinnies and make our way through the drizzle to Mr. Pike, our coach. He's got a dry erase board with our positions marked out. Levon is quarterback; Double X and Coty, wide receivers; and the rest of us are linemen.

The game is ridiculous, with more fumbles, fouls, and incomplete passes than anything else. The slick bottoms of our canvas sneakers glide across the puddles and patches of mud, threatening to dump us on our asses at any moment. On one play, Wilfred catches a pass from Antwon and takes off right down the middle of the field. He's high stepping toward a touchdown, when, all of a sudden, his feet shoot up into the air so high that they're even with his head. He lands with a splat, and the play ends with a pileup on a loose ball.

Levon stands out clearly as the best athlete. He throws blistering passes that only Double X can hang on to; they bounce off everyone else's chests or whistle through outstretched hands. Once, in a pinch, he throws a pass to Freddie, who shrieks and ducks out of the way. Everyone laughs except Levon, who seems to take it deeply personally, as though Freddie refused to accept a handmade gift.

"Man," he says. "Why'd you duck? That was a good pass."

"I don't know how to play football! I told you."

Levon shakes his head sadly. "Then why you out here? Why you got a red pinney on and flags on your belt?"

Coach Pike tells me to get ready to punt. "Drop back and wait for the snap, James," he says.

"What do I do when I get the snap?"

He laughs at my ignorance of the game. "Kick the hell out of it," he says. "That way." He points at the other team's end zone, just in case I have forgotten which way we're going. Double X squats down, and on the count snaps me the ball. I juggle it, trying desperately to get a grip. But the ball seems to have a mind of its own; it dances on my fingertips, threatening to jump away from me altogether. I grab it just before Wilfred rushes me. At the last second, I cut to the right; he changes directions midstride and makes an athletic grab for my flag, but misses. I hold the ball in front of me with both hands, just like Mr. Pike said, and I kick it as hard as I can. It feels like a good one, but instead of a high looping punt like Mr. Pike showed me to do, it dives low and bounces down the field. A couple of yellow players try to get their hands on it, but it skips past them and settles near the goal line.

"Good kick!" Pike yells.

Tony picks up the ball and starts running. He's fast enough to get past the first red players and is at the midfield mark when Levon cuts across the field to snatch his flag. It looks like the two of them are out for blood, going too hard, and when Levon's right leg makes contact with Tony's, it sends Tony sprawling out of bounds and into the fence. All the other yellow players cry foul, and Horvath blows his whistle.

"Excessive force!" he says. "Ten-yard penalty. First down."

Levon looks like he's going to argue, but he knows the rules: anyone argues with a ref, and they're out of the game.

Tony picks himself up and knocks the clods of dirt and grass off his face. He shoots Levon a look that says, "You're dead, motherfucker."

On the next play, Levon intercepts a terrible pass from Antwon and runs down the right sideline, cutting and spinning, reversing directions and, finally, making a ridiculous dive for the end zone, which isn't a real end zone but a rectangle marked off by four orange cones. It looks like he's going to make it, too, up and over Wilfred's outstretched hands. But Tony comes flying out of nowhere. He runs across the backfield, full tilt and with his head and shoulders down, and collides with Levon's airborne body. There is an audible crunch as the ball pops loose and Levon crumples to the ground. Tony stands with his hands at his sides, twitching with readiness. For what, I wonder? He's already trashed Levon.

Mr. Pike is blowing his whistle like crazy in the backfield, but he's too late. Before he can cross the field, Levon picks himself up and slams Tony with a heavy straight punch to the nose. Tony's head jerks back from the blow, and then he starts swinging with both fists.

Horvath has the good sense to push the pin on his radio before working his way into the tangled, swinging, kicking, mud-covered mess of two fighting boys. Then he grabs Levon across the shoulders and under his armpit. With a powerful jerk he lifts the boy off his feet and away from his swinging opponent. At the same time, Pike grips Tony by the shoulder and yells, "Enough!" But Tony hasn't had enough, because he turns around and decks Pike right in the nose.

Across the muddy field, a trio of guards sprints toward the fight, metal handcuffs and radios flopping up and down on their utility belts. Crupier is high stepping so he doesn't get his new boots covered with mud, and the others plunge headlong into the mess. Mr. Eboue and Samson stay to help break up the fight, while Crupier and another guard take us back to the unit to shower and clean up.

When we return to Bravo from dinner, Tony's room is empty. Freddie says he is bound for Penfield Secure. Surprisingly, Levon shows up at dinner.

"How come you don't get sent away?" says Wilfred.

"I don't know, man," says Levon. "I thought I'd be gone, too." He shovels a spoonful of mashed potatoes. "I kind of wish I was."

51

Mr. Crupier pulls Levon, Wilfred, and me during home-work time. "Crupier with three from Bravo to the gym," he says. "Over." The rest of the guys are sitting at their desks working hard at not finishing their assignments. They are a study in pencil-tapping and random page-turning. Bobby hums; Antwon's eyes are almost fully closed, from fatigue or boredom I can't tell; and Coty draws pictures of four-wheelers.

The guard's radio crackles a response. "Copy that, Mr. Crupier."

Crupier unlocks the big steel door and leads us to the main hallway. Automatically we stop and face the wall while a line from Charlie Unit goes by. "Go on," he says when they are past.

Levon says, "Why are we going to the gym?"

"You guys get to see the dogs because you're the only ones who finished your work."

"What dogs?" I say.

"They got a new program with dogs," says Wilfred. "These people bring them for us to play with and stuff. It's cool."

Levon stops in the hallway with a troubled look on his face. "I don't do dogs," he says. "Mr. Crupier, can I go back to the unit? You can give someone else my spot?"

But Crupier doesn't slow down. "Better keep up," he says over his shoulder. "You can sit on the bench if you're afraid of dogs."

"I ain't afraid of dogs." Levon is trotting to catch up. "I just don't like them. They nasty. They lick their privates."

Inside the gym, a bunch of men and women stand waiting with dogs on leashes. There's a chocolate Lab, a couple of golden retrievers, three little gray dogs, and a fat rottweiler. Mr. Crupier points to an old bearded man standing next to one of the goldens.

"James, you're with Max over there."

I'm not sure if Max is the dog or the old man. When I get close enough, I can see that the animal is old, too, because it's got white around its eyes and muzzle. The guy says, "I'm Max, and this here is Apollo. You can pet him if you want, but you don't have to."

The dog looks at me with big sorrowful eyes like he's done something wrong and he knows it. His head is low, but his tail is slowly swishing back and forth.

I put my hand out for him to sniff, just like Louis taught me to do when we were little.

"Apollo is a rescue dog," says Max. "The Golden Retriever Rescue Society took him away from a bad situation."

"Was he beaten?"

Max nods.

"But he's okay now?" It looks like such a nice animal, the kind you'd expect to see in someone's yard watching over a bunch of kids. It's hard to imagine someone could beat it.

"How does he look to you?"

Apollo licks my hand and then lowers his big golden head. When I scratch behind his ears, he kicks his back leg reflexively and stretches. Then he flops down on his side for a belly rub. I sit on the floor next to him; it feels good, running my fingers through his thick soft fur, and I want to lie down on top of him and close my eyes and shut out the concrete block walls and the giant fluorescent lights and the guards with their radios and cuffs. I want to burrow my face into the softness of this old dog and hide, even if it's just for ten or fifteen minutes.

But I don't know if that's allowed or if Max will get mad, so I stay where I am on the floor, smoothing Apollo's fur with the palms of my hands.

"He's a great dog," I say.

"I think so. You know what I like best about him?"

"What?"

"He's been through hell and back, this dog, but he's not mean. Apollo doesn't have a mean bone in his body."

"He doesn't fight with other dogs?"

"Not unless he absolutely has to, no."

"Does he ever have to?"

"Once. I was walking him through town on a leash, and this big Doberman ran through a screen door and attacked him."

I look at Apollo with his head tilted back so I can scratch under his chin. His eyes are closed, and his rib cage rises and falls with each deep breath.

"What happened?"

"They fought. It was a tangle of snapping, flashing teeth; I dropped the leash and got the hell away from them."

"Did Apollo get hurt?"

"Nope."

"How about the other dog?"

"The Doberman? Apollo whipped him good; he needed a lot of stitches."

Max smiles and leans down to pat the dog on his head. I can see that he's proud. "Every creature has a right to defend itself," he says. "That's not mean."

"Have you ever been attacked?" I know it's a personal question, but it just slips out.

Max's thick white eyebrows bunch together. He looks down at his tan work boots, and right away I'm sorry I asked. "Sorry. It's none of my business," I say.

"No," he says. "It's okay. You go on and ask anything you want to. I might not answer, but you still go on and ask."

Neither of us says anything for a long time, but it's not uncomfortable. A few feet over, I can see Levon and the rottweiler in a standoff, looking at each other.

"I was in the army," says Max. "In Vietnam. That's where I had to fight. I don't talk about it much, but now that you ask, I think it's why I love this dog. We've both had to fight a lot, and neither one of us is mean or angry. At least I don't think we are."

Apollo pushes my hand with his nose to tell me that I'm not paying enough attention to him, so I scratch again behind his ears, which he seems to like best.

Crupier puts his fingers into his mouth and blows a loud whistle. "Time's up!" he says. I stand and shake Max's hand.

"Thank you," I say.

"Sure," he says. "What's your name?"

"James."

"Nice to meet you, James."

Apollo stands up stiffly and chuffs like an old bear. He leans up against Max, the pair of them watching me leave the gym.

52

Antwon has said nothing to me since our fight, and I'm beginning to think that Socrates Fortlow was right: if you stand up for yourself, then that's all you can do. You won't ever have anything to be sorry about, because you'll know you did your best. For the first time in I don't know how long, I am relaxed. Even though I lost my stage, I am no longer afraid. Antwon and his boys can call me names or try to fight me, but now I know how to fight back. I can't help feeling proud of myself; it's a totally new feeling, and a good one.

Mr. Samson reminds us that it's time for group. Automatically we move our chairs in a circle and sit. "I want to hear from someone who used his skills this week," he says.

Antwon raises his hand, says, "I did." This is a surprise, because Antwon never participates; he either puts his head down or sits back and sucks his teeth whenever the rest of us talk.

Samson sighs as though he knows he will regret calling on Antwon.

"Okay, let's hear it."

"I used my dick skills when I was giving it to Levon's mother."

All the boys laugh as Levon stands up. His face is a mask of rage.

"You talking about my momma?"

Antwon grins.

Mr. E stands in front of Levon while Samson gets in Antwon's way. If this goes any further, Samson will push the pin on his radio, and then the two boys will be taken to empty rooms in medical to sit and cool off. For the rest of the day, if necessary. And if they still don't cool off, one of them will get switched to another unit. Probably Antwon, since he's been on almost every unit in the facility and is still on level one, which means no privileges.

But with the focus on Antwon and Levon, no one is paying attention to Double X or Coty. Double X picks his chair up above his head. I can see exactly what is going to happen, and for a moment, I think I can stop it. I can throw my body into his and knock him off balance, or just reach out and grab the chair. I could shout to Samson, "Look out! Behind you!" But I don't. I say nothing. I do nothing as Double X brings the chair down onto the back of Samson's head.

It happens so fast! The chair crunches, and the big man falls like a tree and lands on his face. He doesn't even put out his arms to protect himself, like his brain has shut down or something. How can someone so big and power-ful crumble like that?

Then Antwon sucker punches Mr. E in the face and

follows it up with a series of blows that would drop any normal person. But Mr. E stands with a smear of blood underneath his cheek. Double X comes over to help Antwon, while Coty unhooks the keys from Samson's belt.

The other boys are going crazy, like they've turned into animals. They're jumping around throwing gang signs, shouting incoherent war cries. It's impossible to tell whose side they're on or what they want to happen. I don't think they know. For my part I stand mute and dumb, staring at the heap on the floor that moments ago was the strongest man I have ever known. He was nice to me. He taught me how to lift weights and build up my muscles. He told me I was stronger than I really knew. So how can I stand by helplessly while bad things happen? How come I never know what to do? I thought I was done being afraid, but I am still terrified.

I take a step toward Samson's giant unmoving body. If I can just get to his radio and push the small rectangular orange button, the pin . . . I take another step.

"Hey!" someone yells.

Hands grab at me, pulling me away from Samson and his radio. Wilfred tears my shirtsleeve off. Then he jumps on top of a table, pumping his fist in the air while Mr. E faces Antwon and Double X, talking slowly and calmly, but he's also speaking to the rest of us.

"Think, guys," says Mr. Eboue. "You don't want to do this." He turns for a second toward the giant body of his friend, who is still unmoving on the floor. "Samson! You okay, brother?"

There is no answer from Samson. Mr. E is backing up

toward the door, hoping that help will come soon. He hits his own pin, and this time the radio responds almost instantly: "All available staff to Bravo Unit!"

"Come on!" says Coty. He's got the keys and is posted by a window looking out onto the main hallway. "Now!"

And just when I start to think that they might get away with it, Levon comes out of nowhere and clotheslines Antwon with an outstretched arm, sending him backward into the wall. Then Levon dives on top of him, pinning him with his knees on his chest, pounding him in the face with his fists. The blows make solid thwacks.

"Talk about my momma! My momma is a fucking saint, motherfucker! Nobody talks shit about her."

With Antwon out of the picture, Mr. E squares off against Double X, who, all of a sudden, looks unsure. Maybe even a little scared. He takes a halfhearted jab at Mr. E, but the guard pushes Double X's arm away with the heel of his hand and spins him around into an arm bar. Lightning fast, Mr. E pulls his cuffs out, snaps them onto Double X, and pulls him down roughly onto his butt.

"You stay there," he says, breathing heavily. Coty takes this as his cue and bolts out the door into the main hallway. The rest of us watch through the big plate-glass windows as he runs smack into a troop of approaching guards.

Mr. E leans over the body of his friend. "Talk to me, brother. Say something."

53

I count nine guards in Bravo Unit before we are herded, one by one, into our rooms. Coty, Double X, Antwon, and Levon are all on the floor being restrained. Freddie knocks on the heater vent and tells me that soon they will be cuffed and taken away; we will not see them again, though he thinks Levon may get a second chance, since he *did* help Mr. E.

Looking out my window, I see Samson start to move a little bit as a crew of paramedics arrives. He tries to lift his head up, but Mr. E makes him lie back down so the paramedics can put this thing on his neck to stabilize it.

After they wheel Samson away, Freddie says, "This is really bad."

"Yeah." I feel sick to my stomach; I am trying to slow my breathing down so I don't throw up. I hear Freddie talking, but I'm not really listening.

"Oskar's dead. Samson's all fucked up. And you!"

The last part catches my attention. "What about me?"

"What was you thinking, stepping in like that?"

"I don't know. I just did it."

He grunts.

"Did you see what they did to Samson?" I ask.

"I know, but I'm just saying . . ."

"What *are* you saying, Freddie?"

"That those guys are gonna give you shit for that."

And as usual, he's right. Wilfred bumps me in line at dinner the next day and spills my juice all over my food, soaking my hamburger bun and fries. I ask the cooks for more food, but the kid working the steam trays says, "Sorry, no seconds." Then he flashes a quick grin and says, "No seconds for brownnosers and staff pets!" In gym, playing basketball, I get fouled so many times that Mr. Crupier calls the game and sends us back to the unit to our rooms. "Nice job, James," someone says. "Fucking snitch."

The dog people are back, and I get to spend half an hour with Apollo after school. He greets me by pushing his massive golden head into my chest. I am so happy to see him that I have no words for it. I scratch him behind his ears, and rub his belly when he flops down at my feet on the gym floor. I tell him how much I've missed him. And even though it's childish and embarrassing, I say all kinds of stupid shit like "You're my best friend" and "I love you, Apollo."

Max, the owner/handler, tries talking to me. He asks me how I've been doing and when I'm going to get out. But when the tears start rolling down my face onto Apollo's coat, he gives up. They are big hot tears, and they pour out of me so easily, like a valve has been opened. I should try to stop myself, but the truth is, I just don't care anymore.

Maybe I am soft and weak. Maybe I am a crybaby and a brownnoser. I don't care.

"I'll leave you two alone," Max says, even though the handlers are supposed to be with their dogs the whole time. "It looks like you have a lot to talk to each other about."

And we do. Apollo lets me hug him and pet him and cry into his thick fur. When I finally stop to wipe my eyes, he lifts his paw and places it gently on my leg. In the background I can hear Bobby, who has taken Levon's place. His cast is off, and he's playing tug-of-war with the big rottweiler, whose name I gather is Rosie. He is laughing and shouting.

"James," he calls out, "check this out. Rosie's mad strong. Look!"

But I don't care about him or anyone else right now, because my time is almost up and I don't want to leave Apollo, the big shaggy creature who loves me back so perfectly. Max is still sitting on the bleachers, watching patiently, but the next group of kids is already lining up, getting ready for their turn.

Apollo and I both stand; he leans against me so that my hand brushes the side of his head. Then he nudges me with his muzzle, leaning in even closer until I can feel his weight against my leg. We stay that way for several minutes, and I feel strong and safe, like nothing can touch me as long as we're together. It's about the best feeling I've ever had in my short trouble-filled life. Because I know that this dog loves me completely. It's so simple, and I try to enjoy it even though I know it will fade as soon as I walk out the gym doors.

54

Today in Ms. Bonetta's class we get a surprise. "I have an announcement," she says, standing in front of the class, looking shockingly beautiful in a black dress and heels. I've never seen a woman so classy and sexy up close; it makes me feel a little crazy, like I'm dizzy and can't think straight. My body is buzzing even though I know she's my teacher and I am her student, and never in a million years would anything happen between us.

She's smiling, like she's got the best news in the world, something that could cheer up a bunch of delinquent kids and an angry redneck guard.

Predictably, Wilfred raises his hand. "Are you having a baby?"

Some of the guys chuckle, no doubt thinking about the lucky guy who might have gotten her pregnant.

"Wilfred, I'm writing you up for asking personal questions," Crupier says. "You know better."

"Sorry, mister." Wilfred lowers his head, ashamed. Or angry. It's impossible to tell the difference, except that when he's angry, he curses quietly, under his breath, and makes threats. And when he's really angry, he throws his giant shovel hands into the air until the guards restrain him. As long as I've been here, though, he hasn't actually hit anyone; it's more like when a little kid has a tantrum.

"It's okay," Ms. Bonetta says. "It's not that kind of a surprise, Wilfred." She pauses to build the suspense. Even Crupier looks interested; he closes his copy of *Traditional Bow Hunter* magazine and looks up at the pretty teacher.

"One of you boys has just been accepted into community college!" She claps her hands a couple of times and waits for our reaction.

But everyone knows it's Freddie. Wilfred and Kyle wave their hands away to show that they couldn't care less. Even Freddie tries to downplay it by saying, "It ain't a real acceptance, because it's just community college; all you have to do is apply."

Ms. Bonetta puts her hands on her hips. "It *is* a big deal. It *is* an accomplishment, Freddie, because you worked hard to get this far. Isn't that right, Mr. Crupier?"

The guard looks like he's been slapped awake. "Yeah," he says mechanically. "Absolutely. Nice job, Peach." Then he grins stupidly at the teacher, like he expects a reward for talking nice to a poor troubled kid.

"If life is hard," Ms. Bonetta says to the rest of us, "and we don't celebrate the small accomplishments, what's left?"

We all nod like it's the most important thing we've ever heard, but really it's just because she is so beautiful and kind. Her dark wavy hair shines. Her teeth gleam. And even though she dresses professionally and wears buttoned-up sweaters over everything, it is clear that she has an awesome body. Even Bobby, who hates school with a fury, sits up straight, listening attentively like an A student.

I wonder how the waitress from Rusty's or the girl who blew me a kiss would look in a black dress like Ms. Bonetta's. Probably really good, but not so classy and elegant. That would be fine with me, though, because I'd kind of prefer a real girl as opposed to a super classy one like Ms. Bonetta. Someone who is happy going to the movies or for pizza instead of to parties and dances. And it would be great if she liked to read and we could sit by the river and talk about books and movies and stuff. Not that any of this is going to happen. But it's nice to dream.

"So today," she says, "we are all going to celebrate Freddie's success."

She lifts two paper grocery bags onto her desk and starts to pour soda into paper cups. Then she passes around little Halloween-sized M&M's bags and Snickers bars. Wilfred and Kyle say "Good job" to Freddie, but most everyone else sits quietly, eating. Crupier, too, sits in the back of the classroom, pushing M&M's into his mouth, looking hungrily at Ms. Bonetta in her black dress and heels.

55

In the morning Freddie and I are scheduled for showers. Pike unlocks all of the bedroom doors. "Morning, ladies," he says. "Showers in five. Get moving!"

Our small wire baskets hold soap, shampoo, and shaving items, but Freddie's is loaded up with all that he just bought at the commissary, things that only kids with privileges can have: lotion, conditioner, hair gel. We're halfway across the unit floor when Horvath stops us and says, "Wait a minute, Freddie. What's with all the extra stuff?"

"I bought it at the commissary. I got my stage. You can check—I ain't lying."

He scans the unit log for the entry. When he finds it, he slams the book shut and shoves it across the desk.

"Don't get too comfortable," he says. "'Cause I'll be talking to Eboue about this."

Freddie's smile turns to a scowl.

"Go on," Horvath says. "Might as well enjoy them privileges for one day."

Freddie storms across the unit, taking these giant angry

steps; his robe flaps open, and he has to reach around to cinch it back into place.

"Stop!" says Horvath.

Freddie stands in his thin blue robe, looking down at his toes. I know what is going through his mind: if Horvath writes him up for this, his release will get pulled and he'll miss community college.

"The tie on my robe's busted," says Freddie. "I put in a request for a new one."

"Save it, Freddie. Nobody in here wants to see your junk, except for maybe James."

Pike snickers, along with several boys who have come out of their rooms to see what's happening. Ordinarily, guards would send them back to their bedrooms, but today it suits them to have an audience. This way, if they write Freddie up and take away his privileges, there will be plenty of witnesses to back them up.

"It ain't my fault, Mr. Horvath. I swear!" says Freddie.

"It's your job to keep yourself covered up; nobody else's. You know the rules."

"But I'll lose my stage. I'll miss college!"

"You want some cheese with your whine? You ain't going to college anyway. Who are you trying to fool?"

"Yeah," adds Pike. "Maybe you should have thought of all that before you flashed your pussy to everyone."

Horvath laughs out loud at the joke. Freddie clutches his robe tighter while he fights to keep himself under control.

"Get moving, Peach," says Pike. "This conversation is over."

But Freddie doesn't move, and the only sound is the big clock ticking away on the far wall. The rest of the boys stand outside their doors, watching. They'd like to get closer, but there is the risk of the guards turning on them, saying, "Get back to your rooms! Mind your own business!" Then they will miss all the action.

Freddie breathes deep and says, "I don't have a pussy." He says it loud and clear, like it's a declaration, like it means more than what they're talking about at the moment.

"What?" Horvath is puffing up, getting big and red-faced. "Are you talking back, fruit?"

"I said I don't have a pussy, and I'm more of a man than you are."

"Hah!" Horvath grabs his balls and says, "A real man has these; what you got is a pussy."

Freddie's eyes blaze, and his nostrils flare. "Say some more shit," he says slowly, calmly, the words measured out like volatile things that might catch fire or blow up. "And see how bad I kick your fat stupid redneck ass!"

Our mouths hang open in disbelief. Wilfred, smiling, his face lit up, says, "Oh, no he *didn't!*"

Horvath and Pike look at each other, surprised that someone like Freddie would challenge one of them directly. But they are happy, too, because now they have a reason to drop him. They fan out, getting ready for action. But since the riot, they're not taking chances; slowly Pike slides his hand down for his radio and pushes his pin.

"Response Team A to Bravo Unit," the radio says.

"Keep talking, Freddie," says Horvath. "They're gonna love you at Penfield."

226

But Freddie is done talking, and whatever fight was in him is gone. He knows that, any minute, a troop of guards will come in and take him to one of the small rooms in medical. They'll drop him over and over again. And later he will get written up and will lose his stage. His release will be pulled, and then he will miss college. Freddie lowers his head and shoulders in defeat as the sound of heavy black boots echoes from the hallway.

56

I wonder if Freddie is gone for good, like Antwon, Coty, Levon, and Double X. Even if they let him come back to Bravo, he might be all lumpy and beat-up. He might have a broken arm or really bad rug burns on his face. And even if they don't hurt him too badly, he might be broken in other ways, as in being hopeless or defeated.

But at midnight, I hear movement outside Freddie's door. Keys jingle, and a lock clicks open. "Get in there," says one of the guards. I hear the shuffle of Freddie's footsteps; the door closes and locks behind him.

"Freddie?" I knock three times on the heater vent to get his attention.

Nothing.

"You okay?" I speak louder, but he still doesn't answer.

At wake-up Crupier unlocks my door first, and then Freddie's. "Come on, Peach," he says. "It's a new day. Time to man up and fly right."

It takes Freddie several minutes to come out of his

room. And when he does, he has a strange look in his eyes, like he's afraid and not afraid at the same time. It's like he can't decide if he should cower in front of the guard or smash his head in with something heavy. Honestly, he looks crazy.

He says nothing throughout breakfast, and eats his waffles and Frosted Flakes separately, just like everyone else. Later, in class, he refuses to do any work; instead he stares at Horvath until someone tells him to turn and face the front of the classroom. Even then, he does it only for a minute or two—then he goes back to staring.

Horvath stares right back. "All day long, Peach," he growls. "We can do this all day long."

At lunch I ask Freddie what the hell he's doing, but he says, "I got my plan. You'll see." Othe than that, he does nothing in school and sleeps when he's not forced to participate. He has also stopped taking care of his hair, which is wild and uneven.

It's not until the very end of the day, after lights-out, that he knocks on the heater vent. "James," he says, barely loud enough to hear.

"Yeah?"

"They took me to the tune-up room."

I lean back against the heater panel. I'm listening, but I don't want to listen. I want to plug my ears and shout, "Shut up! Shut the fuck up, Freddie!" Because I am tired of this place and I don't want to hear it anymore. I want to go home and never think of Morton again. I want to go back to my mother's crappy couch. I want to go back to school, where I am invisible, except for the lacrosse kids who mess with me in the hallways, which I don't care about anymore because I've learned how to stand up for myself. But don't tell me about the stuff I can't do anything about, like Bobby's broken arm, Oskar's suicide, and what happened to Samson.

"You want to know what they did?"

"Okay," I lie.

"They restrained me over and over again."

"Oh," I say, stupidly.

"They'd pick me up and ask me did I want to go back to the unit? And I'd cry and say, 'Yes! Please, yes!' Then they'd drop me again. And again."

I can hear him crying.

"I peed myself, James. I peed in my fucking pants, I was so scared. I thought they was going to kill me."

"I'm sorry, Freddie."

After he gets control of himself, he says, "If something happens to me in here—"

But I cut him off. "You're crazy," I say. "Nothing's going to happen to you."

"Don't lie, James," he says. "Don't you lie to me."

"Okay." I don't know what to say to make him feel better.

"Just promise me something. Promise you'll find my mother and tell her I'm sorry." He's talking fast now. "Her name's Gwendolyn Peach. She lives in Harlem, in the East River projects. You got to call her and explain things. Tell her I'm sorry for being the way that I am. Tell her I didn't mean to cause her no grief."

"Okay, I promise. If anything happens, I'll find her."

The radiator goes quiet. I lie awake for a long time thinking about Freddie and his mother. I say a silent prayer that he will find his way home.

57

It's Friday, which is Stage Night, but no one on the unit has privileges. We've been on restriction since the riot, and no one knows when it might end. Instead of playing Ping-Pong or cards, we sit in the dayroom flipping through magazines and doing homework. I look around at the empty seats, seats that used to belong to Oskar, Tony, Antwon, Coty, Levon, and Double X. In my head I catalog where they might be. Oskar I know is dead. Mr. E said that Tony, Levon, and Antwon are at Penfield, and I don't know where Coty and Double X are—maybe in a different facility, or in jail.

As for Samson, I try not to think about him. I want to ask Mr. E if he's okay, but I am afraid of the answer. Also, Mr. E is different now, quiet and not as friendly. He did shake my hand and thank me for trying to help him, though. "You stood up for me, James," he said. "I won't ever forget that."

Freddie sits at the next desk over, hands resting on top of a black marbled composition book. His hair is wild and clumpy. The lines of his face are drawn downward with the weight of what has happened to him. He talks little, and when he does, it is only about his "plan."

"You okay, Freddie?" I say when the guards go into the staff office to eat the order of subs and wings and Cokes that just arrived from Central Services.

"No, I ain't okay. But I'm gonna be, after I get Horvath and Pike."

"What are you going to do?"

"You'll see," he says after a moment. "Take this letter and read it." He takes a folded sheet from his notebook and slides it over to me.

"Okay."

"You got to put it in Pike's mail slot in the staff office. I can't do it, 'cause they don't let me in there now."

"I don't know, Freddie. It sounds like a bad idea."

"So what? Just do this for me, and I'll never ask you for nothing again."

"Are you sure?" I don't know what's in the letter, but it can't be good.

"I'm sure. I been working hard to get it right. You know, matching Horvath's writing, the way rednecks talk. You'll see." He laughs, but it's a sick laugh, a little wheezy, like Pike's. "Trust me; you won't believe I wrote it."

"I still think you shouldn't."

"James, I been taking shit from people my whole life. Everybody treats me like a fucking joke. My own parents don't want me. Even the gay boys don't want me. They say shit about my clothes, call me a fat, dumpy-ass Negro with no style."

"Is that why you stole the suit?"

"See, you smart, James. You sit and watch everyone, and you know stuff without having to run your mouth. I'm always running my mouth, which gets my release took away and a bunch of knots in my head."

"It was pretty good, though, what you said to Horvath."

Freddie surprises me with a smile. "Yeah, it *was* pretty good." Then his voice changes, gets deeper, serious. "I'm not taking no more shit, James," he says. "I want to stand up and say, 'This is who I am, motherfuckers. What you gonna do about it?'"

"I know what they're going to do about it," I say.

"Then that's their business. But I still have to stand up for Freddie Peach."

I nod.

"'Cause if I don't, who else will?"

He walks away with his composition book, and I tuck the letter under my arm so the guards won't notice. Later, in the safety of my bedroom, I carefully open it and spread it out on my bed. In small blocky print, it says:

To Byron Pike:

Byron, it's me, Roy. Horvath. I'm taking a risk writing this letter, but I think it's okay—it's illegal to look in someone else's mailbox, and I also know you'd never say nothing to no one because, well, that's how you are—loyal and real decent. So here goes. I watched that movie everyone's been joking about, *Brokeback Mountain*, about them cowboys who are queer but also tough and regular guys. Well, Bryon, that movie got me thinking about your strong face and that bristly red beard, and how maybe there ain't nothing wrong with that, even though I still hate queers, the way they lisp and dress all flashy and stupid. But that's different. I'm talking about two regular guys doing regular guy stuff together, like hunting and watching the races over at Watkins Glen. And we could take trips on my Harley. You could ride bitch until you get your own bike, but you should know that I'd never call you my bitch, because it's not like that. I think of you with lots of respect. Anyway, tell me what you think. We can pound some beers at the Summit Lodge later and talk about it.

I read it three times, laughing out loud, imagining how Pike would react and how much of an absolute shit storm would erupt if anyone else saw it. I call out to Freddie through the heater vent, telling him that it's hilarious.

But all that comes back is, "It ain't no joke. It's payback." And then he adds, "Keep your promise, James, if you're my friend."

I'm pretty sure a real friend would tear up that letter. It's what Louis would do, but only because it might bring trouble for him. But then Freddie says, "Are you still my friend, James?"

"Yeah," I say with a mix of sadness and pride. "I'm still your friend."

58

I carry Freddie's letter with me tucked in the folder of my school binder. Every time he sees me he asks, "Did you do it?"

"No," I say. "Haven't had the chance yet."

"Keep trying. And don't chicken out on me, James. I'm serious about this, and you promised!"

"Shut up," I say, because I don't even want to do it. Because it's too dangerous. Because I'm afraid of getting caught with Freddie's letter. I might pretend that I'm worried about my friend, but it's more selfish than that; if I get caught, I'll never get out of here. And if I do it, I'll be setting up something terrible for Freddie.

I can almost hear the voice of Tony telling me to let Freddie handle his own business. Louis would tell me the same thing. Wolf Larsen, too. There's even a line in the book where he says, "I do wrong always when I consider the interests of others. Don't you see?" Honestly, I don't know what to do, and I can't ask Samson, because he's still hurt. And Mr. Pfeffer is in Dunkirk, a couple hundred miles away.

But in the evening, the perfect opportunity comes. Horvath has gone to Central Services to pick up their take-out order from the sub shop, and Crupier is running chores and showers.

"Wilfred and James," he calls out. "Clean the staff office. And do a good job; I want one of you to dust and then use the spray; the other one vacuums."

Wilfred goes to the slop closet to get the vacuum while I duck into my room to get the letter from my binder, which is on my desk. I fold it four times quickly and stick it into the waistband of my khakis.

"James!" Crupier says.

I duck out of the room. "Yes?"

"I didn't tell you to go into your room; I told you to clean the staff office."

"Yes, sir."

"Go ahead, then."

And I do it. Over the noise of Wilfred running the vacuum and singing his stupid rap songs that don't even rhyme, I put the letter inside my cleaning rag and slip it into Pike's mail slot without anyone noticing. There are butterflies in my stomach, and I feel strangely elated, like I've just set something in motion that can't be stopped. It is a powerful feeling, and I wonder if it's how Wolf Larsen felt when he drove his ship, the *Ghost*, into a squall, knowing that the sails would be ripped to shreds and the men swept into the sea to drown.

Is this how it feels to destroy something? To start something powerful and destructive, and then sit back and watch it explode? I clean the rest of the office and then go to bed. I'm too nervous to sleep, but I don't want to do any more push-ups or squats. At least not until Samson comes back, if he ever does. I lie on top of my covers and throw a balled-up pair of socks at the ceiling and count how many times in a row I can catch it. I'm up to fifty-seven when Freddie raps on the heater.

"I'm up," I say.

"Did you do it? When you was cleaning the staff office with Wilfred?"

"Yeah," I say.

"For real? Don't lie to me, James. Please don't tell me no lies."

"I'm not lying. I did it."

"Good," he says. "What do you think Pike will do? When he finds it?"

"I think they're going to live out the gay redneck dream. You know, taking trips on Horvath's Harley, drinking beer at NASCAR races. Can't you see it?"

"Hell, no! Them two got no style and they talk like retarded farmers. They think corn dogs is fine cuisine."

"And they have more hair on the back of their necks than on their heads," I add.

"That's right," Freddie says. "So they ain't allowed in the club."

We laugh and joke about the ridiculousness of it. It feels good to have the old Freddie, my friend, back. But there's a part of me that feels like I'm talking to a dead man, or a ghost, because soon enough Pike will start his shift and find that letter. And then more bad things will happen. Then again, maybe he won't find it. Maybe it will get lost, or he will think it's a bad joke from one of the other guards. He could just throw it away and never say anything.

But I know that deep down I am fooling myself; neither Freddie nor I have that kind of luck. For us, the shit storm is right around the corner, and the only question is, How long? Will Pike find the letter at the beginning of the shift, or after? And will it take minutes, hours, or days for him to trace it back to Freddie and me? It doesn't really matter, I guess. Just like it didn't matter for Van Weyden when he finally realized he was on a hell ship and everyone was going to die.

59

In the morning it is quiet except for the ticking of the big wall clock outside my door. It's half an hour before the end of Pike and Horvath's first shift (they're doing a double: eleven to seven followed by seven to three), and nothing bad has happened. The electric locks retract. Pike opens our doors with his usual brisk efficiency and trademark comments.

"Good morning, ladies," he says. "Time for hygiene. Chow line's in forty-five, so get the fuck up and fly right!"

After hygiene, we get in line behind Horvath, who is washing down a sausage, egg, and cheese biscuit from McDonald's with a swig from his giant coffee mug. We stand quiet, rubbing the sleep out of our eyes just like we'd do on ordinary school days, days when there isn't a forged letter sitting in Pike's mail slot in the staff office. I wish it could be one of those days.

In the cafeteria Freddie is all smiles and jokes. He bobs his head like he's grooving to music only he can hear.

"What the hell are you doing, Peach?" Pike says.

I give him the eye to make sure he won't say anything stupid, but he ignores me, grinning even more broadly.

"Just enjoyin' my breakfast, Mr. Pike," he says. "It's delicious."

"Well, cut that shit out!" Horvath says. "Just eat your food."

Freddie nods and crams the rest of his breakfast burrito into his mouth.

Wilfred touches his own chin and says, "You got salsa on your face."

"Oh, yeah? Well, lemme tell you something, Wilfred. Shit's going down today. I can feel it."

"What are you talking about?" Wilfred says.

"I'm just saying I got a feeling that shit's going down today, and when it do, nobody gonna care about no sauce on my chin."

Wilfred gives a short nervous laugh like he does when he's not quite following the conversation. "Whatever," he says. "Just so long as it don't involve me, 'cause I got, like, six good days behind me. I'm gonna get my stage."

Freddie winks at me because it's funny how Wilfred is always "gonna get his stage." For ten months he's been counting his good days, only to blow it over something stupid like stealing extra desserts at dinner, or writing gang signs on his school desk.

"That's good," Freddie says. "And don't worry, Wilfred; it won't involve none of y'all. It might even be fun to watch."

Wilfred smiles.

60

All day I watch the clocks for the end of Horvath and Pike's last shift, which is at three o'clock sharp. At one-thirty, I am cautiously optimistic. At two, I'm hopeful. And by two-forty-five I am overflowing with relief because Crupier is coming in to get ready for the switch; he throws down his duffel bag and then leaves, probably to get a coffee or something from one of the vending machines in the break room.

A loud noise from the staff office stops my heart, but it's just Horvath's big deep laugh. Laughing is a good sign. Everything is still okay.

Freddie is watching, too, but I know he's hoping for a different outcome. He wants to see everything explode, like when Tony picked a fight with Levon. Or when Antwon and Coty and Double X attacked Mr. E and Samson. I try to think of a future for myself in which things don't explode. Could it be that I will walk out of here one day soon and go home? It's possible, but I haven't heard or seen from Louis in weeks, and there's almost no chance of my mother's apartment passing a home inspection. Mr. Eboue talked to me about it; even if Ron isn't around to mess things up, state law says that there has to be a separate bedroom for me—and there isn't.

Another loud noise from the staff office, but this time it's not laughter.

"I didn't write it," says Horvath.

"Then who the fuck wrote it?" says Pike.

Oh, shit, I think. They got the letter.

"I . . . I don't fucking know, Byron!"

The two guards move into the dayroom, shouting at each other. They shake fists and roll their heads at the ceiling because they think the letter is real. Their stupid redneck world has just been turned upside down, and I have to appreciate the genius of Freddie's plan. He hit them where it would hurt most—their masculinity. They're glaring at each other now like the lunatics on reality shows who are only one step away from choking the shit out of each other.

Horvath roars, "You think . . . you think that I'm . . . ?"

"I don't fucking know what to think, Roy!"

And then Freddie does his thing, what he's been waiting to do for so long: he lights the fuse. He stands up, slowly extending his arm in front of him. He points his index finger at the two guards and says, "Hah!" It comes out like a statement or an accusation. But then he says it again, differently, like all he's doing now is laughing at something funny. "Hah! Hoo-hah!"

Horvath takes a step toward him, confused, but also dangerous.

He says, "The fuck are you laughing at, Peach?"

"You," Freddie says, dropping the loaded, pointed finger. His smile is gone. He looks serious, not at all like the happy funny Freddie I've known since I came to Morton. But there's something else that's different about him—I just can't pinpoint it.

Horvath takes two more steps on his big tree-trunk legs. "Why are you laughing at me, fruit?" he says. "Tell me."

Everyone in the room is watching, waiting for Freddie's answer, and I know what's different about him. Freddie has become a man. He is making his stand, just like he said he was going to do. He is becoming strong. I don't know how long it will last, but for the moment, Freddie Peach owns Bravo Unit. I watch like the other boys, openmouthed, awestruck.

Slowly, in clear measured tones, he says, "Watching you and your boyfriend have an argument is funny."

I can almost see the gears turning in the broken machinery of Horvath's mind. His eyes turn black and cloudy at the same time, like the sky on the cover of my paperback, a sky that threatens to rain down and smash anything underneath it. I know that we're not on a ship and there is no water around us, but I can't help wonder how long before my friend is cast into the sea.

61.

There's a terrible moment when Horvath and Freddie face each other, seething hate. Horvath breathes deep, his massive chest expanding until finally, all at once, he expels the air and slams down on Freddie's shoulders with both hands. Freddie flies backward and crashes onto a desk that's covered with homework papers, and the big, heavy staff logbook.

Horvath stands his ground, nostrils flaring like a bull. He says, "You weak faggot sack of shit."

Freddie picks himself off the desk. He notices the logbook, raises it above his head, and hurls it. Horvath sees it coming and ducks, the book sailing past him, thudding against a wall. But it is enough of a distraction that Horvath fails to notice Freddie take a small step forward, planting his weight solidly on his left foot like a boxer ready to jab. Nor does he see Freddie's right foot draw back so far that we can all see the waffled pattern on the sole of his fake Chuck Taylor shoe. By the time Horvath knows it,

Freddie is driving the shoe as hard as he can square into the big guard's balls.

Horvath lets out a single grunt and drops hard to the floor. He lies on his side, knees curled, coughing. He crams his hands between his legs protectively, a low moaning sound coming from the twisted sagging flesh of his face.

Peals of laughter escape from the other boys and me; we are surprised at Freddie's boldness and his accuracy. "Maybe that boy should play football," says Wilfred. "Special teams and shit."

Freddie stands over Horvath, taunting him. "Who's the faggot now?" he says. He winds his foot up again, ready to deliver another blow, this time to Horvath's face. But Pike jumps into action. He knocks Freddie off balance with a shoulder block and hooks Freddie's arms behind his back. Then, in a smooth, practiced motion, Pike slides his right leg over the front of Freddie's left leg. He levers him up and over his hip, pitching him onto his face. Freddie's glasses crack and fall off; his lip splits and he lets out an epic string of curses that makes Wilfred and Bobby laugh in appreciation. Blood and saliva spray from his mouth with each curse.

Just three feet away Horvath makes it up to his knees, a line of drool running off his chin.

"You okay?" Pike says, barely controlling the kicking, thrashing body of Freddie.

Horvath staggers to his feet. He ignores the question. "He's mine," he says, wiping his chin with the back of his hand.

Pike levers up Freddie's arms so Horvath can slide into

the primary position. Horvath takes the arms and puts his full weight on top of Freddie's back. "Fucking faggot," he says, squeezing, torquing the arms.

Freddie's face is mashed into the carpet, eyes wide with pain; he screams, "Don't! You're hurting me!

"I'm sorry," Freddie says. "Whatever you want from me, I'll do it! I don't care no more. Just get off me!"

The boys of Bravo Unit shift nervously from foot to foot in flip-flops and their own fake Chuck T's. We grimace whenever Freddie screams. Several boys throw gang signs, mutter curse words, and shout incomprehensible things that can only be the language of brutality, a language that is becoming too familiar to me. I see all of this now as inevitable, unstoppable. It's like the scene in *The Sea Wolf* where the cook is dragged behind the boat and everyone knows what is going to happen. Everyone can see the shark fin cutting through the water like an implement of destruction, an agent of destiny. What started out as a joke (to give the foul-smelling cook a bath) quickly turned into a matter of life and death. That's how it seems here, too, because Horvath is the shark, and Freddie is dangling from a rope.

The guards' radios stay clipped to their belts. The orange pin buttons remain un-pushed. And there's no one who can help. Crupier's still getting coffee, Mr. E hasn't come in yet, and Samson is still recovering. I take the smallest step forward, but Wilfred is keeping an eye on me. He grabs my shirt and says, "You ain't going nowhere."

Freddie is whimpering now. His face is flecked with blood and tears and saliva. "I don't care anymore!" he says. "I ain't going to college anyway."

247

He stops fighting, and his body goes limp, drained of anger, drained of the energy to fight back. But if Freddie has no more energy, then Horvath has too much; he is fueled by his own hate and blinding stupidity. He jacks Freddie's arms up even higher, so that his chest is directly over Freddie's shoulder blades and he is shouting directly into Freddie's right ear.

"I don't care anymore, either, faggot. You hear me?"

Freddie is silent now, except for the occasional sob, and I start to wonder if Horvath might actually kill him. Is it possible to kill someone in a restraint? Mr. E said a boy was killed at the place Mr. E was locked up in; maybe this is how the boy died.

I look around at the other boys to see if they notice what's happening, but they, too, have gone into fight mode, where kicks and blows are the rule, and you don't even need to take sides. Wilfred lets go of my shirt and pumps his arms in the air, hooting, cheering for more violence. These boys were happy enough to see Freddie trash Horvath, and they're just as happy now that the tides have turned. Maybe Wolf Larsen was right, and life is simply a mess. Maybe the strong eat the weak so they can stay strong. Maybe that's all there is.

Where the hell is Mr. E when I need him? Where is Mr. Pfeffer with his ice-cold root beer and his books? What good are they now? Useless, just like me and my immobile limbs, and the muscles that Samson worked so hard to help me build before he got struck down by a chair.

62

A deep sound fills the air around my head. It's a low,
growling note like the sound of the small-block eight-
cylinder engine in Louis's old Bronco, and it builds, growing, accumulating power, rising in pitch until it is shrill,
piercing, and finally I can identify it. I know what it is—a
war cry. A fucking war cry! And still it's building, roaring
above the stupid din of Horvath and Pike and Freddie's
insufferable noise.

But before I can figure out where it's coming from,
my body is in motion and I am on top of Horvath's back,
punching at his head and the side of his face. My fists are
light but potent, blazing fast; I don't even care where they
land, just so long as they move and fly and blur the air between him and me, proof that I am no longer immobile,
no longer inert, no longer complicit in my silence and in-
action. I am not the quiet, frightened boy sitting on the
sidelines watching. I am finally doing something. I have
made my choice.

Horvath tucks into a ball for protection. He covers the

back of his head and neck, and I remember Tony's advice on fighting—get in close and go for the body. So I change up my punches and beat as hard as I can on his back. I swing wildly; most of the blows glance off harmlessly, but a couple of them drive home in the soft spot below the back of Horvath's rib cage. He howls and rolls onto his side.

At the same time, Pike gets off Freddie and grabs me from behind. He puts me in a choke hold and squeezes hard, like he really means to strangle me. I try to shake free, but he's got me, tightening the hold every time I move. I can't speak, either, because his arm is pressing on my throat and it hurts too much, like my Adam's apple is being crushed.

It is surprising how quickly I become dizzy from pain and lack of air. But I have a clear view of Horvath staggering to his feet, pawing at the right side of his face, which is red and blotchy from where I hit him. This gives me grim satisfaction, and I only wish I had hit him harder.

Horvath lurches closer, and I can see that there's something wrong with his eyes: they are looking at me and focusing, but there's nothing inside them. It's like Horvath himself, the angry, sweaty McDonald's-eating guard, is gone. Even the mean part of him—that thought he could beat the gay out of Freddie or smash Pike's dream of becoming a pilot—is gone, replaced by a staggering grunting animal who wants only to destroy me.

He's not able to see me now as I truly am, as I have finally discovered myself to be— James, a fifteen-year-old boy who is going to get out of this place and make a life for himself. I am not James the boy who wanted to be a man but didn't know how. And I am no longer James the gullible boy who believed what everyone told him because it was easier than thinking for himself.

It's okay if Horvath doesn't notice how I've changed, how I am changing. Why would he? He's stupid, and blinded by rage. His mind has been turned upside down by a fake gay love letter, and beatings by two people he underestimated as being soft and weak.

He grabs me roughly from Pike and barks, "Leave him."

Pike sees the craziness in his partner's eyes and lets Horvath take over the choke hold. The big man's hands are hot, too hot, like there's some kind of terrible energy in them. He grabs my wrist with one of his big hot hands; I try to throw him off, but he is too strong, too crazy. He wrenches me around and hooks my arms so violently that it feels like they're going to pop out of their sockets. Then he wrestles me over his hip, and I hit the floor on my face. He presses his weight down on my back, pinning me. I try to fight, but I can only move my face from side to side, rubbing it raw on the coarse gray carpet.

I try to speak before *all* the air leaves my chest. "Stop! I can't breathe!"

Horvath presses down even harder on my back, which I didn't think was possible. How much does he weigh? How strong is he?

"Fucking liar!" He slurs into my ear. "You're breathin' enough to talk," he says, "you fucking liar."

I want to tell him that it's not true, that I'm not a liar. I might be naïve, but a liar I'm not. It's true that I'm not getting enough air; little inky dots are floating across my

251

eyes. It's true that there's a weird pressure noise inside my head, like the sound a teakettle makes when you shut if off and the steam is tapering. It's also true that I deserve this, because I didn't do anything when Samson, a great man who was my friend, got struck down by a punk kid who believed in nothing.

I stop fighting so I can focus on breathing, but Horvath is too strong. He is too heavy. It's like I am being pressed in one of Mr. Goldschmidt's woodworking vises, the steel faces of the vise squeezing out my life as the big wooden handle turns slowly around. Freddie's a few feet away curled up on his side crying. And I can see a row of white canvas sneakers, the boys of Bravo Unit playing out their roles, standing, watching, being pushed and pulled by the invisible waves of hate and anger that keep surging through the facility.

I gasp one more time for air.

And then, nothing.

63

I awaken to a guard's voice. "Is he faking?"

Now a woman's voice, maybe the nurse's. "He's got a pulse and he's breathing."

"But is he faking?"

"I don't know, Byron. Probably. You know how these kids are."

She waves something sour-smelling in front of my nose. I shake my head slowly back and forth to drive away the smell that shoots into my nose with a sharp pain.

"Put him in the shower for a minute," she says. "Then you'll know if he's faking. Bring him to the clinic when you're done."

Hands are touching me but not in a violent way. I am being rolled onto my side; it feels good, easier to breathe. But something isn't right, and it's hard to get things in my eyes to focus. A large shape that must be Horvath paces in the background, looking agitated. Another dark shape leans close and whispers into my ear. It is Mr. Eboue, and I am happy he is here. Now everything will be okay.

Nobody gets hurt when he and Samson are around. I wonder where Mr. Samson is. Maybe he's on vacation or pass days. I should know, but I can't remember, just like I can't remember what happened for me to be lying on the floor. Maybe I was restrained again, or maybe I got into another fight with Antwon. Yes, that's what must have happened.

"James," Mr. E says, all calm and nice. "You okay, my man?"

I want to answer him, to tell him yes, I'm fine, just tired. But I can't get the words to form, and then the Horvath shape is shouting at the Mr. Eboue shape, something about it being his restraint and he'll finish it, not nobody else. Pike jumps in and yells at Mr. Eboue, too. Mr. E backs off, saying, "Take it easy, bro."

"I ain't your brother," says Horvath.

"I know, I know. Just take it easy, okay?"

Next thing I know, I am being lifted to my feet by Horvath and Pike and guided across the dayroom to the showers.

"Cold water?" Pike says.

"Yeah," says Horvath.

The cold spray against my face feels good, like rain, and I smile. I close my eyes and open my mouth to taste it. I haven't felt rain since the day I got arrested, and that was more like mist than rain.

"See? He's faking," Pike says. "He thinks it's funny."

"Keep laughing, asshole," Horvath says.

They pull me out of the rain and drag me across the dayroom floor, toward the door and the hallway beyond.

"Wait!" Mr. Eboue runs over with a pile of something

254

in his hands. "Dry clothes," he says, but Horvath swipes at them and knocks them to the ground. Now we're moving down the hallway toward the clinic. They have me firmly by my shoulders. My right foot drags behind me like an anchor, and I laugh a little bit because it reminds me of Wolf Larsen's ship, the *Ghost*, when it wrecks toward the end of the story on Endeavor Island, masts and rigging dragging over its side. Maybe I'm like a ship, only one with torn rigging and a cracked compass. The liquid is leaking out, and the needle is spinning wildly, because I don't know where I am going or what is happening to me.

In the clinic a small white shape—who must be the nurse—pops off a few pictures of the side of my face. Maybe I've got another rug burn, but it doesn't hurt. Nothing hurts, really, and I want to tell her this so she'll know I am okay. Maybe then I can go back to my room and go to sleep.

"You learned your lesson yet?" she says.

I don't understand what she means, but I am so tired. I am too tired to ask her to explain, so I just agree.

"Yes," I say.

"Don't be smart," a male voice says. But I am closing my eyes to get some rest, and I can't see who the voice belongs to. Horvath again, probably.

"Why is he in wet clothes?" she says.

"'Cause he was faking. Manipulating," says Pike.

She sighs, hands me a pen, and says, "Sign right here."

I try to write my name, but it's like I don't have full control of my hand; it only does half of what I want it to. I drop the pen and look at a spot of scribbles.

"That's not your fucking name," Horvath says. He picks up the pen and puts it in my hand again. "Last chance before you hit the floor again."

"It's okay, Roy," the nurse says. "It's legal. Take a seat and we'll get this over with."

Horvath drops heavily into a chair. The nurse starts the post-restraint interview.

"James, do you know why you were restrained today?"

"No. I mean yes. I don't know." I close my eyes again to rest. So sleepy.

Strong hands grip my shoulders and shake me awake. "Listen!" says a rough voice.

"Okay. Listening." But I'm not sure if I've said it in my head or out loud.

A quieter voice, the nurse's, says, "Tell me why you were restrained, James." She sounds angry, though. I don't think she likes me.

"Why was I restrained?" I honestly can't remember.

"You have to tell us, James."

I think hard, but all that comes up is Wolf Larsen's ruined ship. "I have a cracked compass," I say. "I don't know where I'm supposed to go."

"What is he talking about?" the nurse says.

"He's full of shit," says Pike.

"Yeah, I've had enough of this bullshit. Byron, gimme a hand; we're done here."

But the nurse interrupts. "Wait, guys. Let me finish." She says, "James, do you have any injuries from this restraint?"

"No."

"Are you sure?"

"No."

The nurse drops her clipboard and pen with a loud sigh. She's frustrated, but I don't know why. I'm pretty sure I answered all of her questions.

"Bullshit!" Horvath shouts. He grabs me by my arms and takes me to a small empty room. It has bare white walls, and a white linoleum floor. I think it's the place Freddie told me about. What was it called? The tune-up room. I can't remember what he said about it, though, other than it's a bad place. It's so hard to think, but I'm pretty sure I shouldn't be here. I need to get out of here.

"Is this the tune-up room?" I say.

"There *is* no tune-up room," Horvath grunts as he hooks my arms and takes me down to the floor.

"Yeah," says Pike. "Because you're still in the clinic. With the nurse."

Falling, I feel as light as a child. I want to put my arms out like I did on the handlebars of Louis's BMX bike. I want to yell, "I am king of the world!" But I can't, because the air rushes out of me when I hit the floor. I gasp for breath. My head is spinning, and I am overcome with a feeling that, inside me, something terrible is happening, but even that doesn't last, because the weight on top of me crushes it, crushes everything, crushes me into the floor like the whole world is on my back and is going to drive me down through the floor and into the earth. What will become of me when I am pressed into the earth? My face twitches once. Twice. I close my eyes to sleep.

64

White-clad paramedics run alongside the gurney, guiding me through the electric gates of the facility and across the parking lot, to where a helicopter waits. They are careful even though they're in a hurry, and I want to thank them, maybe tell them not to go to so much trouble for me, because I feel fine despite what has just happened. I am not worried, or afraid. One of the men puts his hand on mine and says, "Hang in there, buddy. You're going to make it. I swear you're going to be okay."

I want to say something to reassure him, but I can't talk because my breathing is thin and shallow, and it's all I can do to keep my eyes open and look at the helicopter blades hanging down at their tips, all wobbly and half-assed. I wonder how something so fragile-looking can fly, but when the rotor powers up, the blades become a cyclone beating the air down and flattening me to the gurney, until the men fold up the gurney legs and slide me into the helicopter.

"Just hold on, buddy," the guy says again. I try to smile to let him know I'm okay, but my face muscles don't work.

I can move my eyes, though, and I look out the windows, which are all around. A tornado of dirt and leaves swirls outside, twigs and bugs and other dried-up things riding the currents of air. And I am flying. I look out the window and down at the gleaming metal roof, and the razor wire that shimmers in the sunlight. I don't know how it's possible, but in my mind I can see what's going on inside the facility; all hell has broken loose. Response calls ring out on every unit: three restraints at the same time on Alpha; a riot on Charlie; and boys banging on locked doors on Bravo, cursing, threatening to bust their way out even though that's not possible. Freddie bangs, too, with a new kind of rage growing inside him, one that will carry him far away, toward his mother, Gwendolyn Peach, and college, and all the nice clothes he's dreamed of.

Mr. Eboue sits in the staff office with his head buried in his hands, while Horvath paces behind him, intermittently punching the wall. The Sheetrock has given way in the shape of a fist, a symbol of his rage that will stay for weeks, until the maintenance men come with a bucket of Spackle and a roll of tape. They'll do it under order from the director, who wants the place shipshape for the team of dark-suited investigators (the same ones who visited after Oskar's suicide).

"This place is fucked up," one of the maintenance men will say.

"Fucked up," the other will echo, slathering too much mud over the dent, which will take forever to dry and will probably crack.

I see these things as they are happening, even as I rise

higher in the helicopter. It's like the shimmering layer of heat and air over the green metal roof is giving me special vision. And I can see farther away, too. As we fly higher, I follow a slow-moving line of pinpoints on the highway to a place in the distance where Louis is helping my mother into his crappy little car. She looks frail and sick, and he holds her arm for support.

"I didn't even call," she says.

"I know," Louis says.

It's the first time they've spoken in more than two years, and she is filled with sadness and shame and other poisonous things. She's gotten the call from Morton to let her know that I'm in a medical helicopter; she doesn't entirely understand, but she knows it's bad and thinks it's what she deserves. She feels gray and used up, not even capable of tears.

But the tears are already welling, threatening to spill out and glide down her cheeks. They will be the soundless kind of tears, the ones that don't announce themselves with the heaving, racking mechanisms of a breaking heart, because she is past that, she thinks. A mother like her, she tells herself, hasn't the right to beat her chest and cry out. But she doesn't know that she *will* cry out, and that her tears will wash away some of the grayness, at least enough so that she can look at her other son, Louis, and see him as he truly is: another boy pretending to be a man, unsure of everything except his white-knuckle grip on the Honda's steering wheel, and the pressure of his foot on the gas pedal as he speeds west on I-90 toward the hospital I am being taken to.

"Too many bad things," they say to each other.

"I'm sorry," I try to say, but I can't form the words, and as I watch them, I realize they are crying because they think it is too late. And it *is* too late, at least for me. But then the last thing I see before I close my eyes is my brother loosening his fingers from the smooth plastic shifter and taking my mother's cold brittle hand in his. He holds it and drives while I smile inwardly, thinking that maybe there are such things as second chances.

Author's Note

The title *Kindness for Weakness* comes from a phrase I heard hundreds of times during the years I worked with boys in New York's juvenile justice system. Those three words were invoked to explain behavior that might appear to outsiders as narcissistic, violent, and even sociopathic. But to the boys, "kindness for weakness" was more than an explanation; it was a rule, part of a code that taught them that acts of kindness made them look weak, a code that helped define their manhood. If they followed the code, they earned status and respect. And if they didn't, they risked becoming outcasts, getting beaten, or worse. Harsh, yes, but for boys who were raised by single mothers and grandmothers, boys whose fathers and uncles were either dead or in prison, this code represented all they had to guide them toward manhood.

I wish I could offer an apology for the fact that this is such a sad book. If you've finished it and have some dark lingering questions, then this is where I should rattle off frightening statistics and shout for reform. I should tell you that James's story was inspired in part by actual events in a facility where I worked . . . events that affected me enough to set in motion the slow-moving gears in my head that sometimes, after a thousand or so revolutions, lead to the creation of characters and stories. I should make a profound point, leave you with something beyond the observation that for some people—people like James and Freddie—the world is a hostile place.

But to be honest, I'm not sure I have a point other than that, in the face of violence, showing kindness requires tremendous strength and is often punished severely. That's a terrible point, if you ask me, but one that deserves close study. It's certainly a turn from *Something Like Hope*, my first book, about an incarcerated girl named Shavonne, in which acts of cruelty were tempered by moments of compassion and understanding. True, those moments were few and far between, but they were enough. And when I finished writing and editing the book, I felt complacent for a little while. I took a new job at a public high school. I turned my attention to a book about a wild road trip that had nothing to do with troubled kids and broken systems. But as time passed, the voices of James, Freddie, and the others began to demand that I tell their story. So I did. And instead of apologizing for the darkness of this story, I will simply thank you for reading, and thinking, and feeling. Thank you, sincerely.

Shawn Goodman is a writer and school psychologist. His experiences working in several New York State juvenile justice facilities inspired *Kindness for Weakness* and his first book, *Something Like Hope,* which won the 2009 Delacorte Press Prize for a First Young Adult Novel. Shawn lives in New York with his wife and two daughters.